CARLYLE SIMPSON

CARLYLE SIMPSON

KAREN LEE OSBORNE

ACADEMY

CHICAGO

Published in 1986 by
Academy Chicago Publishers
425 North Michigan Avenue
Chicago, Illinois 60611

Printed and bound in the USA

Library of Congress Cataloging in Publication Data

Osborne, Karen Lee, 1954–
    Carlyle Simpson.

    I. Title.
PS3565.S43C37   1986   813'.54   86-3313
ISBN 0-89733-184-2
ISBN 0-89733-204-0 (pbk.)

ONE

DUFFY'S FUNERAL

On the day of Duffy's funeral Carlyle did not arm-wrestle. He mowed his lawn, front, back and sides, emptied the grass and carted it down the street to the vacant lot where he would later burn it. His was the finest lawn in all of Garfield Estates, sweet Argentine Bahaia, thick, and deeper green than the waters of the Gulf. He knew for a fact that there were more blades of grass per square inch on his lawn than on any other. His lawn was the prettiest, the healthiest, because he worked harder than anybody else. Problem was, most human beings, even if they did have two eyes in their heads (and he knew several who behaved as if they did not), could not or would not, out of sheer orneriness, realize that it took plenty of hard work to keep that lawn pretty.

Duffy knew. Duffy had been one of the few, an honest man who pretended to be nobody but who he was. Retired from his hardware store before Carlyle himself had retired ten years ago (ten years early, some said), he had lived all alone in a single-wide at Trailer Haven. Duffy never said much, but he knew. He was the only man in that trailer park who rode a bicycle instead of a giant tricycle; he would bicycle back, raising his hand to his straw hat for any ladies he happened to see, whether or not they were wearing their teeth. He could outdrink just about anybody in Johnny's, except Carlyle. Then he would complain about the noisy young people who had somehow been allowed to move into the trailer park, but usually he said little. He never raised his voice or spoke real filth, at least not that Carlyle could remember, but he never seemed to be upset when others did. Carlyle smiled as he thought of scrawny old Duffy listening to all kinds of goings-on at Johnny's, most of them shouting matches and arguments over football games. Carlyle knew his own voice was probably the loudest, and his talk could be dirty, though there were others who could tell dirtier stories about women these days.

The bright sun glared in his eyes. If Duffy had complained some about the trailer park, Carlyle knew he himself had done more than his share of griping about Helen and everything else. Well, Duffy was gone now. Couldn't go back and do it any different.

The motor was running steadily beneath him; its noise surrounded him; a drumming like the drumming in his head he couldn't get away from. No reason to subject himself to noise and this heat except that he wanted the job done right. He could let that brat down the street do the mowing, and it would only cost six dollars. He could be like everybody else on the block, but he wasn't; they called him crazy to stay out here at his age in the Florida sun just after twelve o'clock noon cutting his own grass, but by God he had never in his life let a lawn boy do his work for him and he wasn't going to begin any such foolishness now. When his back began to act up he had bought the riding mower, but that was the only concession he would make. Once a week he took the big rusty rake down from its hook in the garage and ripped up all the ugly St. Augustine that kept creeping over his property line from the Methodist minister's yard next door. He hated St. Augustine and he hated that smooth-voiced minister, who paid the boy to cut the front and let the back turn to weeds as high as the grapefruit sagging on his trees.

Duffy had told him once recently to quit complaining about that minister. It wasn't like Duffy to say a thing like that. It seemed now, looking back, that Duffy had *said* more things near the end, things that were sometimes hard to figure out. Did Duffy know, somehow, that he didn't have much time left?

Tiny streams of sweat coursed down Carlyle's neck under the hot sun. One thing, the old guy hadn't waited until near the end to start going to church; he had started that when his wife died about a year after he retired. They used to kid him in Johnny's sometimes about riding his bicycle to church. Usually you could kid Duffy about anything. He was a good sport. But he didn't like people taking liberties.

One Sunday afternoon a bunch of neighborhood guys — some from the trailer park — were watching TV at Johnny's: the Miami Dolphins were playing somebody or other. Just about everybody, except Duffy, hated Miami. But the Dolphins were winning, and everyone was sore. During the commercials one of the guys started needling Duffy about his prayers being answered. Duffy didn't say anything. He didn't even smile. Anybody could see that Duffy wasn't in the mood to be kidded about going to church; Carlyle could see it and he had already had several bourbons and water. But the loudmouth kept it up, without looking at Duffy. He said he saw Duffy huffing and puffing to church on his bicycle, and he figured they must be serving real wine there — like the Catholics — because otherwise why would the old man bust his ass to get there? Get plastered with God's blessing.

Everybody thought he was funny, except Duffy and Carlyle.

"I don't reckon you ought to talk about being plastered," Carlyle said. Although he knew that Duffy, who rarely showed it, had drunk more than anyone that afternoon.

"Hey, hey, Carly," Nelson said. Nelson was a young salesman who could work his own hours. He was good with people. "Nobody meant anything."

"Churches just make Carly nervous," Johnny said from behind the bar. His white teeth flashed against his olive skin. "He probably hasn't seen the inside of one since his wedding day. Once burnt, huh, Carly?"

They laughed nervously. They had all heard Carlyle complain about Helen.

"No, seriously," Johnny said, "I for one know that Carlyle really appreciates Helen's church. It gets her out of the house one day every week."

Someone murmured that he wished *his* wife would go, and the conversation trailed off when the game continued. Duffy had not said a word. The Dolphins scored another touchdown right away.

The memory of that day was strangely vivid out here in the bright sun. He had felt uneasy, wondering whether Duffy had approved of his speaking up that way. He kept his gaze on the grass ahead and cut the swaths cleaner and neater than the lane lines on highways. He still wondered what Duffy was thinking, but he would never know. No sense in dwelling on it. He leaned over the edge of the mower and spat.

"Carlyle! Don't you want to come in out of that hot sun and have some lunch?" Helen was calling from the house in her mild Southern accent, ever so polite, but always nagging about his health. He ignored her and went on working. There was nothing wrong with his health. She was the one — didn't smoke, took maybe one fancy cocktail every six months — Helen was the one who had to keep running to doctors about one problem after another. She had just turned sixty, he realized suddenly, a couple of weeks ago. Years ago he had stopped remembering her birthday with gifts or dinners or any of that. Now he had to remind himself that she was actually five years younger than he was; he thought she seemed much older.

Sweat crept along his forehead, toward his eyes. If he let it go, it would drop into his eyes and burn like hell. But he kept both hands on the steering wheel, cut close to the trunk of the tall pine and swung sharply to straighten for the next swath. His right eye began to burn. Sweat was always sliding past the brown leather band on his straw hat. He increased the speed and cut a close, even swath through the sweet-smelling grass. He turned and cut another, following the high, unmown ridge with precision.

Another turn, another ridge, and it was time to change the grass carrier. The mower had a special attachment that collected the grass as you cut. If that dead stuff spread out all over the lawn while you mowed, it would choke the healthy grass, and after a while the lawn would thin out and look like everybody else's. He drove over to the cement driveway and stopped. He tried to stand up, but his back ached; he was stiff. Carefully, bent over, he stepped down. The carrier was almost full; it was heavier than he had expected. He grunted and heaved, throwing his shoulders and his aching back into the effort to pull it off the machine.

None of them realized what hard work this was. Helen didn't; she was basically lazy. There she was shuffling out again, her shapeless housedress flapping around her flabby, useless body. He looked at her floral print bedroom slippers and felt like spitting on them. She had a big ham sandwich waiting for him, if only he would come in out of the hot sun and eat it. He was asking for a stroke, she said. Asking for a stroke or a heart attack and it would serve him just right if he got one — he didn't have to go out in the hot sun to mow the lawn; he could just as easily have done it in the morning when it was still cool. When he did not answer she retreated into the house.

Grunting, he hauled the carrier over to the wheelbarrow, lifted and heaved it over the edge. The truth was he mowed in the direct sun because then the lawn was driest and cut closer. Afterwards he always gave the lawn a thorough watering. If he was asking for a stroke Helen was asking for a belt in the mouth. As if he'd never done it before. She did not understand that what a man needed after working in the hot sun was not a big lunch but something cold to drink, and lots of it. Beer was the best thing. Sometimes he had actually gone inside and picked up the plate with the ham sandwich and thrown it against the kitchen wall, but still Helen did not seem to understand. Oh, she would give him beer, too, but it was never cold enough. Inevitably, he would end up slamming himself into the driver's seat of his big white Ford and driving to Johnny's.

He rested against the wheelbarrow, holding the empty grass carrier, for a moment before he walked slowly back to the mower. He would empty the carrier five more times before he was through. Three wheelbarrows full of dead grass to be burned in the lot at the end of the street. Every week he burned the dead grass he had dumped there the week before. The burning he would leave until later. He always went to Johnny's as soon as he finished mowing.

He cut the last swath before two o'clock and turned on the sprinklers. Helen came out again, this time bringing a large glass of iced tea, still trying to get him to eat lunch. He drank the tea, knowing it wouldn't quench his thirst.

"You don't need to go to Johnny's today, do you, Carlyle?" she asked in her polite, frightened voice. He kept drinking and then crunched on an ice cube. "Not before the funeral anyway. Or are you going with some of the other men?"

He shook his head. "No. Hadn't planned to go with any of them."

She drew in her breath. Her dress flapped at her knees. "I don't suppose you want me to go with you?" she asked slowly, as though she were afraid to ask.

"No." He did not suppose he wanted her to go.

"I'll pray for him." Hesitantly she put her hand on his shoulder.

It was strange to feel her touch; she did not often touch him. Usually she shrank away from him as soon as he entered the room.

Now her hand was on his shoulder, so lightly that it seemed to tremble. He shrugged it away.

"You don't need to pray for Duffy."

"I just thought —"

"I'm going out," he said. He left her sanding there with that look that said, All right, be ungrateful. Go off and leave this nice sandwich I fixed for you.

He wanted something cold; he wanted to sit, dirty and sweaty as he was, and drink cold beers. Helen was always worrying about what people would think, always whining. "Couldn't you at least put on a clean shirt — you've been wearing that one for two days." At Johnny's nobody cared how he looked or how he smelled; they knew he worked harder than all of them. He had been going there for years just the way he was and he had done just fine. Helen could look down her uppity nose at them, but these "ungenteel" people were his friends.

He was glad to see that Vicki was tending bar. She was a good-natured woman with puffed-up platinum hair, and she smiled at him when he came in, showing her pretty white teeth. Helen's were gray, like his.

"Nice cold Bud comin' right up, Mr. Simpson. You look right tuckered out." Vicki knew how to treat a man.

He eased himself slowly onto the backless stool at his usual place at the bar. Vicki put the bottle and glass in front of him, and he poured the beer carefully against the side of the glass so it would not foam up.

"Hey," he said, "why doesn't Johnny get some stools with backs on them?" He had asked this before, but sure enough Vicki was good for a smile.

"Darlin', if we did that, you'd get so *spoiled*. You don't want us to go around spoilin' people, do you?"

He grunted. They thought it was a joke, but it wasn't funny. Those stools were hard on a man's back; he had to leave the bar and sit at the nearest table. He took a long, steady drink of the beer and felt better. When he set down the glass, a hand clapped him on the shoulder.

"How you doin', you old fart! Ready for some wrestlin'?"

It was Nelson, his old buddy. Carlyle shook his head.

"We got a funeral this afternoon," he said. "Remember?"

Nelson sat in the chair opposite Carlyle and rolled up his sleeve. He still wanted to arm-wrestle, on the day of Duffy's funeral. But Carlyle told him he wasn't about to do any such thing. Duffy deserved more respect than that. Nelson shrugged. He flexed his right arm, and then rolled down his sleeve. He was forty-five years old, and tanned from golfing, fishing and working in the sun. Anybody who looked at him would call him a strong man. But Carlyle, twenty years his senior, could beat him arm wrestling. Not so easily that he could brag about it, but every time, when he set his mind to it. Each time he pinned Nelson's arm to the table while somebody else counted to ten, he felt calm and satisfied. Nelson was a good sport about losing, so Carlyle let him win once in a while, just to keep him interested. He could beat Nelson today if he really wanted to. But he did not want to. Maybe a guy Nelson's age couldn't understand.

Vicki brought him another beer. Nelson got up and went over to a group of kids at another table to try to con one of them into wrestling. The cold beer tasted great. It wasn't healthy to sit in air conditioning like this after working in the sun, but it felt so good. It was too expensive to run air conditioning at home, but it was something else to be able to come in to a place like this and drink cold beer in comfort. Sometimes he stayed at Johnny's for hours on hot afternoons like this, but today he did not want to stay. The place reminded him too much of Duffy. He could see him sitting there, complaining about the trailer park and the noisy punks who had just moved in. Maybe Duffy had died complaining. He was just an old man who could be a good sport, or who sometimes complained a lot, or often just sat there without saying anything. Probably no one would miss him. Except Carlyle.

He left the money on Vicki's tray and pushed abruptly out into the heat. His car was stifling, the steering wheel was burning hot. He gripped it with one hand, and backed up to turn into the narrow road behind Johnny's, the road which led to Duffy's trailer park. Down a narrow lane hardly wide enough for his car, past five or six trailers — some of them pretty big — and then Duffy's. He stopped the car. This was where Duffy had lived. The rusty bicycle was propped against the trailer, the blue boat sat in the carport. There was nobody there; Duffy's sister from Atlanta was going to sell the trailer.

It was an honest trailer; it didn't pretend to be anything but a trailer. Silver, with rounded corners — it looked like a tin box. All trailers were tin boxes, but most of the ones in trailer parks were big and fancy, wide as houses. It was horrible to think of a man dying alone in a trailer; a man should die in his own house, with his own land under it. Some land you could sell, but not the land you lived on.

Back in 1950 Carlyle had been far-sighted enough to buy up quite a few acres on the beach, and now that was one of the most valuable pieces of property in the state. It would provide for their old age. His daughter had kicked up a hell of a fuss when she found out he had sold it to a developer. "More high-rise condominiums out there," she said. "Ruining what's left of a beautiful beach . . . you've made sure it will be ruined." But there were no complaints from her when he paid for her college education; that was all right with her. The way she talked, she would rather have seen him sell his own house and land than that beach property. But he would never sell that; he had built that house himself and he had made that lawn the best in the neighborhood. The best houses in town had been built by Carlyle Simpson.

Nowadays the contractors were all skimping, worse than ever: walls you could put your fist through, crummy baseboards, cheap plastic in the bathrooms. His houses always had good porcelain and solid walls. Ten years ago he had built what he thought was his last house, but now he was going to build one more. He had found a plan that had knocked Harold Beaumont off his feet. The plan was at least twenty years old, the architect wasn't even around any more. But the minute Harold had finished looking it over he had said, "That's the house I want, and I want you to build it for me, Carly."

So they made a deal. He had told Duffy about it the day before Duffy died. He was going to build one more house. It was nice of Harold to make it possible, but Harold or no Harold he had intended to build another house anyway, because he wanted to show

people what a well-made house was like. New people were jumping
to buy shoddy constructions: they thought they were beautiful, they
thought they were in good taste. Ha. Like he said to Nelson once,
"It would be better if they went ahead and holed up in one of those
tin boxes." He said it without thinking; he forgot for a moment that
Duffy was sitting there. But it was true, and Nelson and Duffy both
knew it. Duffy knew what he meant. The new houses were no
better than trailers. He spat out the window, backed the Ford out of
the lane, and headed for home.

Helen came into the garage when she heard his car pull in.
"Carlyle, don't you think you should change? You don't want to
wear shorts to a funeral."
He grunted and put the rake in the wheelbarrow filled with
grass.
"Well, you *said* you were planning on going. I just thought I'd
remind you."
"Doesn't matter whether I go or not."
"Of course it does."
He stared at her. *Shut up,* he thought. She was all ready to start
gabbing. He wasn't going to let her use Duffy's funeral as an excuse
to dress up in her Sunday clothes and do her Christian duty so that
everyone could say that Helen Simpson was a good Christian
woman, it's too bad about her husband, isn't it. And he sure as hell
wasn't going to let her tell him what he should wear.
"Carlyle, of course I didn't know Duffy Mills as well as you did,
but I *know* that he certainly would have gone to *your* funeral, if it
had been the other way around."
She was reminding him that Duffy went to church. If she started
telling him that Duffy was in heaven now, he was sure he would
have to stop himself from bringing the rake down on her head. But
all she said, in her soft feathery voice, was, "You know that as well as
I do."
She stood there watching him as he guided the wheelbarrow out
to the driveway. He heard her sigh as he headed out to the street.
Let her go ahead and worry until the last minute. First he was
going to burn the pile of dead grass left from last week, and then he

would change his clothes. He pushed the wheelbarrow down to his vacant lot, and heaved it onto the pile of fresh grass. Then he walked over to the pile of old grass. The sun was still high, but he hesitated before lighting the fire. Was it too windy? He looked at the houses next door and across the street. Old Mrs. Martin's car wasn't in her driveway, so she wasn't watching out for him. It was a good thing she wasn't around; she was always complaining about the grass burning — said she couldn't get the smell out of her house. She even threatened to call the police. Let her try. He was damn well going to burn what he wanted to burn on his own lot whenever he damn well pleased.

When the blaze was going well he almost wished he had not started it. The wind was strong. He used the rake to keep the flames from spreading. He knew how to keep the fire under control; no one should be afraid of fire who knew how to do it right. He could picture Helen watching him from the kitchen window, one eye on the clock, worrying about whether he was going to change before the funeral. Always worrying about silly things. He did not know why she was like that, but she was. Maybe she was a good mother, but by God she could drive a man crazy. Worrying that he might wear shorts to Duffy's funeral. But what did she know about Duffy? He was the one who knew about Duffy. He was the one who had gone on all those fishing trips with Duffy — that was a lot more important than a stuffy funeral and shorts or long pants. Duffy loved to go fishing; nearly every day he pestered Carlyle to go with him. But Carlyle turned him down a lot. He really didn't know why, now. He would say that he had to mow the lawn, or he had to take Helen somewhere, or his back was bothering him. But he could have gone with Duffy. And nearly every other time he had refused.

That last fishing trip was caught in his mind, a hook that would not come loose. They had been out all day in Duffy's little sixteen-footer. The smelly catch was scattered between them. The sun was going down and they were tired. It was time to turn the boat around and head for the marina. Duffy's face was drawn; he looked sick.

"Carly," Duffy said. He turned up the brim of his hat and stared at Carlyle. "What's the most important thing in the world to you?"

At first Carlyle wasn't sure he heard right. But Duffy kept staring

at him, waiting for an answer. The boat was still. Then Carlyle felt a
tug on the line. A big one. And again. He fought it until the fish
played itself out, and then reeled it in, nice and slow. When the fish
wriggled above the water it looked big enough to keep, but he was
surprised to see that, reeled in, it was a pretty small mackerel.

"Well?" Duffy said.

He didn't know what to say. "What'd you want to ask a question
like that for?"

He cut the hook loose.

"Oh, no reason," Duffy said. "Just wondering. Hey, look at that,
will you?"

Duffy pointed to the west: big grey clouds stretched across the
sky, leaving a clear sliver above the horizon. And there the sun was,
the last moment before it would plunge out of sight. Its orange rays
spread out like a fan, broken by the clouds and refracted upward.
The color of the light turned from orange to pink, then a pale
magenta which grew paler and paler until only the faintest outer
bands of color remained. In the still silvery surface of the water
Carlyle could see the shadows of the boat and himself and Duffy,
and their rods and hats. Slowly darkness fell. He could make out
Duffy sitting unmoving opposite him.

"Hey, Duff," he said, good-naturedly, "snap out of it, huh? Time
to go home."

But Duffy did not move.

"Let's go get some beers, okay?" His words dissolved into the
silence, and he felt stupid. Finally he reached over and touched
Duffy's shoulder.

"Duffy?" he said. His voice did not sound like his own. "Are you
with me, old buddy? Time to go."

Slowly, Duffy responded.

"Sure. Sure, Carlyle. Time to go."

But Duffy's voice did not sound right. Quickly Carlyle set down
the rods and tugged hard at the motor cord. He was glad to hear the
roar of the outboard, to smell the heavy fumes in the salty air, to see
the propeller churning the still water.

So Carlyle did not answer Duffy's question. What was the most
important thing in the world to him? Was that something a man

should know? If he had to decide, he could not choose the obvious: it wasn't Helen or the house, or any house, and it wasn't the kids. He couldn't think of any particular thing that was more important to him than anything else. He had worried about it for awhile, and then given up. But now that Duffy had died he thought about it again: why had Duffy asked such a question?

He stood resting, his hands clasped over the top of the rake handle, his hat brim pushed low over his downcast eyes. The fire had gone out. He raked the ashes back and forth, again and again. Then he hefted the rake onto his shoulder and walked back to the garage.

He stood with Nelson and the others in his musty blue suit. It was too heavy for this climate. Duffy looked prettied-up: his cheeks were rosy and he looked clean, much too clean and prissy. When the minister's sickening, soft-headed tribute was over — Duffy would have hated it — and shovelfuls of dirt were being thrown on the coffin, Carlyle's spirits lifted.

One by one the men took their leave and drove away. When the last one was gone, Carlyle got into his big, white car and turned the key in the ignition. He drove over to the Rod & Net and parked. He and Duffy had often gone there for a drink when they came home from a fishing trip and did not feel like going to Johnny's.

He sat at a table in the corner and ordered a bourbon. That crazy Duffy, dying on him in the middle of a bet. Somebody had said that Duffy had died because he was afraid to bet on Carlyle any more. That wasn't funny. Well, anyway, Duffy wasn't around any more to care one way or another.

He drank to Duffy — half a toast, half a curse. He knew that people were saying — behind his back — that Duffy had drunk himself to death, just as surely as if he had had cancer or pneumonia. That's what they were saying: that Duffy's doctor had told him to stop drinking or he would die from it. But Carlyle knew better. It wasn't just drink that had killed Duffy. The drink was maybe a symptom, but it wasn't the sickness that killed Duffy.

He ordered a piece of broiled fish. It was good — not like Helen's fish — and he was hungry. A small group had gathered around a nearby table, where two seated men were arm-wrestling. Carlyle finished his meal, and they were still wrestling; neither seemed close to giving in. They were young men, with the red arms and weathered faces of fishermen. Carlyle ordered another bourbon and when it came he got up and took his glass over to where he could watch without getting in anyone's way.

"I'd wrestle either one of those kids and beat him," he whispered hoarsely to a man next to him. "Only I'm not wrestling today." The man looked at him and smiled. "No, really," Carlyle said, "I could. I got people betting on me all the time, just for fun. But they usually get something for their trouble."

"If you wanna bet, you better say so," the man said.

Carlyle realized he was feeling a little drunk. He could feel his face grow hot. He tried to estimate the strengths of the wrestlers, but he couldn't see much difference between them. He shrugged and took out a twenty dollar bill. "The one facing the bar," he said. The man nodded. Carlyle ordered another bourbon for himself and a scotch for his new friend.

Later he could not remember who had won, or any of the loud jokes he knew he had insisted on telling, or how many times he had gone to the bar for bourbons and scotches. It was late when he left; Helen would be listening for his car in the driveway, so that she could heat up his dinner at a moment's notice. Fine. Let her wait a while. She would heat his dinner at ten o'clock, at midnight, if he wanted. So instead of going home he went to Johnny's. He was damned if he knew why he did that. Tomorrow Helen would give him her "so-you-went-out-drinking-again-last-night" look. What did he care?

At Johnny's he sat alone and ordered a bourbon. He did not see anyone he knew, and he did not speak to anyone. He stayed until he was the only customer left, and watched the night barman, Larry, stand all the glasses upside down to dry, and then polish the bar. It was comforting to watch that familiar movement — Larry's white cuff and the white cloth moving back and forth; comforting to be alone and enjoy Larry's respect for silence. Larry would not try to hurry him. If he wanted to he could linger for another ten minutes over the last quarter ounce in his glass.

But he decided to go. He put his last twenty-dollar bill on the
bar and slid off the stool. As he went out the door he heard Larry say
quietly, "Night, Mr. Simpson," and he shrugged in reply. The glass
and metal door felt unusually heavy; it slipped out of his grasp and
shut with a loud clang.

The automatic garage door closed behind him. He struggled out
of the Ford and kicked the door shut. In the kitchen his place was
set at the table, complete with a glass of tea in which the ice had
melted hours earlier. In the dim light he ran his finger around the
rim of the glass; it felt greasy. He threw the glass at the wall. As he
stumbled away, he heard the tea splashing and the glass crashing to
the floor. He knew that if he touched any counter surface or any
dish, he would feel the same thing: grease. Helen grew grease in
the kitchen the way he grew grass in the yard. He couldn't stand it.
The woman did not see well, so maybe it was not her fault, but he
hated grease and he hated especially to feel it in his own house.

In the living room the light was still on; the television blared
static and Helen was snoring away on the couch. She had waited all
night to fix his supper. An impulse to strike her made him hesitate
before he turned off the tv set and the light, and left the room.

At last he reached his own bedroom, where Helen would not
bother him. He stripped off his underwear and pulled back the bed
covers slowly, being careful not to bend much. His back still ached,
even after all that bourbon. He eased himself into bed and lay there
tense; he could not fall asleep right away. He flexed his arm muscles. Tomorrow he would wrestle Nelson and that new young kid,
too, if they wanted, and beat them both.

And tomorrow he had to begin making phone calls. The prelimi-
naries were over; it was time to get on with the house for Harold
Beaumont. The permits were posted, the footing was poured. Now
he had to pull them all together: the electrician, the drywall man,
the carpenters, the workers. Ben Starritt was the best carpenter you
could get; he had always worked for Carlyle. He hoped he could still
get him.

The extras would cause all the trouble: the apprentices, the
young construction workers. They all wanted so damn much money
— more per hour than he had earned in a day when he started. They

would be worth it, maybe, if they were good workers, if they weren't long-haired lazy bastards. Just the other day Helen had said that Bob was not lazy, he was a good worker. She said Carlyle should be proud of him. His son, the construction worker, who also happened to smoke marijuana — or worse. All right, sure, he could work on this house, but if he didn't work out the kid would be out on his ass.

Let him work on trailers, not houses, little tin boxes where people sat alone and waited to go fishing, trying to ignore the young noisy ones who moved into the tin boxes next door. So what was the difference? Carlyle lived next to a Methodist minister who let the weeds take over his back yard and creep over into Carlyle's — no, even drunk, Carlyle was not alone: he could hear the rise and fall of Helen's snoring from the living room. Sometime during the night she would awaken and stumble to the garage to see if the Ford was there, and then would bump along to her own bedroom. And when he married her, her waist had measured twenty-two inches, her movements had been graceful. He closed his eyes, saw the vague shapes of planes he had flown for the Air Force years ago, the vague outline of the chicken house on the farm where he grew up, and the already vague outline of Duffy's face as he sat in his boat, oblivious to all around him. And then something sharp: Duffy's pinched, anxious expression, and the words: What is most important, Carlyle? He could not answer the question because he was not certain that anything was important anymore.

TWO

LEFTOVERS

He woke to the smell of frying bacon. It was late already, almost eight o'clock. Helen would be coming in to wake him up any minute. She would know he wanted to get an early start this morning. Slowly he eased out of bed, and felt little pain. If his back gave him no more trouble than this he would be grateful. He hurried to the bathroom, took a quick shower and got dressed. In the kitchen Helen, in one of her innumerable faded flower print housedresses, was stooped over, washing a brown stain from the yellow wall. The rag she was using was dingy. He had mixed the colors himself for that wall, as he had for all the rooms in the house. Just the palest, most delicate yellow and he had put it on himself better than any house painter you could get around here. He watched Helen stubbornly scrub at the strange stain. She succeeded in removing it, but streaks of water remained, like the dirty grey dishwater she always left in the sink. He could already see, surrounding the area where the stain had been, the beginning of dullness caused by a residue of grease. He shook his head in silence and sat down at the table where Helen had placed his coffee and scrambled eggs with bacon. As he ate the eggs, the toaster popped his Roman Meal, browned only on one side. Nothing ever worked really right in Helen's kitchen, although she had more appliances than he could imagine anyone needing. She turned the pieces of toast over and put them back into the toaster to brown. She waited, tapping her fingers nervously on the countertop. When the toast popped, she quickly jerked the pieces out and brought them to him, apparently oblivious to the heat which must be burning her fingers.

Then she sat down opposite him. The newspaper was folded next to her tea and her own cold toast: every morning she sat, reading the newspaper, drinking her Lipton and dipping her toast in it. She folded the toast in half and dipped one end in her teacup; she ate the soggy part and then slowly dipped the rest.

This morning she did not read her paper. And the crossword

puzzle was blank. She pretended to be looking out the window, but her breathing told him there was something on her mind: she seemed to breathe loudly, in half-caught sighs, whenever she was upset about anything. He could hear her breathing now, all the way across the table, and his hearing was not the best in the world either. Probably she always breathed like that, because she was overweight, but he only noticed it, or could not help noticing it, when there were these awkward silences which always seemed to precede some kind of scene. Often her face would have that burdened martyred look that said, "Notice me. I am suffering." But he saw through it, he knew it for what it was: a woman's self-indulgence. She had everything she wanted, and she did not have to work and if she was suffering it was her own damned business. She continued to breathe loudly and he sat more and more rigidly, determined not to look at her.

He chewed his bacon quietly, using the good teeth on his left side, so that he would not make any noise and attract her attention. Probably she was upset because she was thinking about her old friend Elaine; she knew Elaine from her working days on the Hill. Elaine's visit last month seemed to have jarred her into a period of self-pity. Maybe she was thinking she should have stayed on the Hill. But she had been gone from it so long that she probably forgot that she had been only too happy to leave that little secretarial job when he married her.

She noticed that he had finished eating and got up to bring him more coffee.

"Carlyle, why don't you go by Bob's today and tell him about the job?"

She did not successfully disguise the fear in her voice. Normally he enjoyed watching her tentative attitude toward his own unpredictable reactions. But today he was thrown off: he should have known that it was the children, and not Elaine, who had her in a state. She was wondering whether he was really going to hire Bob as a construction worker on the Beaumont house. She sat down at the table again and, after a moment, saw that he was not going to answer, and went back to her Lipton and her breathing.

He had already decided to use Bob, and he had told Helen that he intended to use Bob, but he knew she did not trust him to remember his promise. She was afraid he would have second thoughts and change his mind at the last minute, just to hurt her. He knew how she tormented herself and sometimes that made him want to let her go on doing it. He finished his coffee, set down the scratched blue plastic cup, pushed back his chair and stood up.

"No need to see him yet. He won't have to start work until next Monday at the earliest."

It took most of the morning to take stock of materials, go over cost changes with Beaumont (how everything had gone up!), and check out what had been done so far on the site. The floor had been poured but had not yet settled; he would check it again tomorrow. The rest had to wait. It was past eleven o'clock when he finally got back to his desk to begin making phone calls. That went pretty smoothly: they all knew he was building the house for Beaumont and they were expecting him to call.

The only snag came when he called Ben Starritt. His wife answered and she said that if Carlyle hadn't been through with the business for ten years for no real reason, why, he would have known that Ben didn't see well any more, and that he had stopped working three years ago. She said he should go out to the Wilson site and see couldn't one of those carpenters help him.

The Wilson site was in a new neighborhood where the town was expanding to the east. He didn't care for these "subdivision" houses, five or six structural patterns to choose from: style 101, 102, 103, 104, 105, in pastel yellow, lime green or pigeon gray. Variations A, B or C—see all the choices you got, ma'am. He could do without any of these people's choices.

Carlyle slammed his car door and adjusted his straw hat, "Well, if it ain't old Carly Simpson!"

That was Bud Rogers who had been a laborer ten years ago. Carlyle was surprised to see him here, a bigwig for Morris Brothers, the firm that handled this area. He had never thought the scrawny worker had it in him. Bud swung his skinny frame over the porch and came up to Carlyle grinning. His small grey eyes darted back and forth.

Carlyle looked at the ugly house. "Looks like you're about through here," he said.

Rogers squinted at him, and kicked a rock down the driveway.

"You looking for help on Harold's place?"

Beaumont, Carlyle almost said, you don't call a man you hardly know — a man like Beaumont — by his first name. But he caught himself. It was Duffy who had hated younger men calling him by his first name. He wanted to be just Mills to them. He didn't care about *Mister,* but he didn't want a lot of cheap phonies calling him by his first name or a nickname either. But Carlyle had never much cared when the boys called him Carly. So why should he care what they called Beaumont?

"Carpenter," Carlyle said. "Looking for that carpenter used to work with Starritt."

Rogers nodded, squinting. "You mean Scovill. Sure, he did this one. His kid is finishing up. You need him soon?" Carlyle just waited. He knew that Rogers would already have heard that the footing had been poured. "Yeah, Scovill's probably your man. He's stopping by later to pick the kid up. Maybe you want to wait, look around —"

Carlyle cut him off. "Yeah. I'll look around."

Rogers went back to work, and Carlyle inspected the house carefully. He examined everything that he thought Scovill might have done. There was something funny about the way the carpenter finished his beams. Carlyle climbed up and down ladders and ran his forefinger along the beams, the wainscoting, the baseboard. He could not check out what was underneath, but he could see what was on top and he knew from that that Scovill did not have Starritt's eye. With Starritt, everything fit. Never a gap, no uneven surfaces or rough edges. Starritt's eyes could see straight lines, curves, any shape you wanted, in the wood. And Ben Starritt's hands knew how to follow his eyes. Probably no one, even a carpenter trained by Starritt, like Scovill, could ever match that fine eye and that precise workmanship.

In the kitchen, the cabinets had already been installed. He opened them and felt along the places where the wood met the wall. Some of the doors stuck; one did not clear the oven hood and could not be used with any convenience. And the wood was not flush with the wall in all places. It was a rough job; even the corners weren't smoothly finished. Nothing like Starritt. The kid was planing doors at the hesitant pace of an apprentice. Carlyle watched him for awhile, holding his hat as he leaned against a counter. He decided he wouldn't wait. The kid did not know who he was, so he could leave without having to settle for Scovill. He could look around some more.

Walking through the house again, he made it almost to the entrance when he found himself looking Scovill straight on.

"Finding all the rough edges, Mr. Simpson?"

Scovill had a wicked streak in his eye, as though he knew something Carlyle didn't. He stood with his arms folded across his chest, a tall, broad-shouldered man, a good head taller than Carlyle. A clump of curly blond hair poked out of the neck of his tee-shirt, and a pack of cigarettes was wound up into the sleeve. Carlyle did not have anything to say to Mr. Rodney Scovill.

"Hear you need a carpenter?"

Carlyle didn't reply, but instead focused on the kid planing the dining room door. He wished Scovill would just take his kid and leave.

"Reckon you noticed I didn't leave the smooth edges like Starritt did for you. All I gotta say is this, Mr. Simpson. You got these houses, they want 'em done by the end of spring, and they don't bring you your graded plane or cypress when you need it and you end up with three weeks and rough edges. Cabinets that stick. Don't think I don't know it. I ain't ashamed of my work, Mr. Simpson, Ben Starritt taught me, but he never had to put up with the shit I've had to put up with, either."

Scovill hitched up his beltless, wrinkled blue jeans, and walked over to the kid. Scovill did not seem old enough to have a teen-age kid; he dressed like a kid himself. Carlyle watched them, not sure whether he ought to take the trouble to answer Scovill. The kid put down the plane and glanced at Carlyle. In a shy, soft voice, he said, "Are we gonna work for Mr. Simpson?"

"Ask *him*," Scovill told the kid. "Ask him who else he's gonna get now old Ben's not around."

Carlyle didn't like the kid looking at him, waiting. He left without saying anything, carrying Beaumont's still carpenterless house inside his head.

He watched Nelson's face turn from red to purple, all the way to his thick, dark hair. He could feel Nelson's forearm begin to weaken. He always knew the moment Nelson weakened; he knew he had him then, before he slowly forced his arm down to the table. The thing about Nelson was, he wouldn't give up. He knew too when Carlyle had won, but he went on resisting every inch. That was the great thing about wrestling Nelson. You got the edge on him and he didn't cave in. He fought hard, with his veins standing out as if someone had slid straws under his skin; the blood must be rushing everywhere just below the surface. Carlyle wondered if his own face were as flushed as Nelson's; it probably was, right up to his grey roots. They were both sweating like pigs. Nelson's hand grew slick and clutched his own hand until the pain made him wince. Their sweat mingled in the pocket of their palms: Nelson clung like a succubus, his powerful fingers crushed his own, but Carlyle smiled because he had Nelson two-thirds down. Then someone gave a short, sharp laugh; in the split second that Carlyle was startled, Nelson almost regained the perpendicular. The *nerve* of that bastard, laughing like that! Angered, Carlyle brought his arm down hard, an instinctive punch. He heard a quiet gasp, of relief rather than pain, but he wasn't thinking about Nelson now. He wanted a word with the loud laugher.

He left the table, but the man who had laughed was a stranger, and he decided not to approach him. Somehow, the guy reminded him of Mr. Rodney Scovill who thought he was such hot stuff. A couple of Duffy's buddies had gathered at Nelson's table when he went back. Vicki was serving them from a trayful of beers.

" . . . rough on her," one of them was saying. "He was her only brother." Carlyle sat down. Two of Duffy's trailer park buddies; he didn't know them well.

"Listen, Carlyle," the speaker said to him, "that sister of Duffy's wants to see you before she goes back to Atlanta. She was going to try to call you at home today. Did you —"

"Naw, too much work to do. I was only home for a few minutes, and I was using the phone some. She say what she wanted?"

"I dunno. Something about giving you some stuff of Duffy's. Maybe you ought to go by and see her. She's at the Holiday Inn on the highway. She's leaving tomorrow, isn't she?"

The other man nodded. "Yeah. If I was you Carlyle I'd get on over and see her."

Carlyle nodded. He didn't want to seem eager. He finished his beer slowly and then got up, and slapped Nelson on the arm. "Good fight for a young'un," he said, and they both grinned.

Duffy's sister seemed all right. She was dressed decently, not too flashy, in a navy blue dress with a jacket. She looked as though she had just had her hair done. It was blue gray. At the funeral he hadn't noticed how blue her hair was. The air conditioning in the lobby of the Holiday Inn was too cold.

"Hello, Mr. Simpson," she said, graciously, warmly. "It's good to see you again."

He nodded and shifted his weight from foot to foot. He felt tongue-tied.

"I hope the next time we meet it will be on a happier occasion," she said. But she was business-like, as though she had put it all behind her now. She handed him a manila envelope and gestured to him to open it. Duffy's boat registration and his keys were in it, along with a fifty dollar bill with a note clipped to it that read, "Don't forget to lay down $50 on Carlyle for the match." Duffy had written a reminder to himself.

He looked at the sister and felt himself blush. He knew women like this hated gambling.

"Uh, this note," he said. "This fifty dollars." But he didn't know what to say. "It wasn't an ordinary bet. You see, down at Johnny's . . . that's this restaurant . . . Duffy and I, we ate there sometimes . . ." Why didn't he just stop? It didn't matter what Duffy's sister thought. He crumpled the bill and the note and stuffed them into the envelope. But he couldn't stop. He told her the match was a fund-raiser for a sick old man who had no family and needed an operation. She didn't blink.

"I know you were a good friend to Samuel," she said. He wished she wouldn't say anything, so he could leave and not look at her after he told that whopping lie. "I'm sure he felt he owed you more than he could repay by giving you this little boat." She went on talking, while he scratched the stubble on his face and tried not to listen to her. She was ruining it, didn't she know that? Dammit, why did women always have to ruin it like this? Duffy's trailer had been moved, but the boat and its trailer, she said, were still on Duffy's lot. Yes, he said, he knew where that was, he would go and pick them up. Awkwardly he shook her hand, and did not realize until the glass door closed behind him that he had not taken his straw hat.

He drove to the trailer park with the windows down to let in the warm, humid air. His white cotton shirt stuck to his back; his undershirt was soaked through. The sun set his vision to a strip of the road between the white hood of his Ford and the glare of the cars ahead of him, so many of them with out-of-state license plates, tourists clogging the lanes. Why he had bothered to lie to the woman he did not know. She was going back to Atlanta tomorrow and he would never see her again, so what did he care what she thought? Duffy was dead so it didn't matter. Anyway it was done with and all he had to do now was hook the sixteen-footer to the car and take it on home. Helen would have her say about the thing taking up her side of the driveway, but she could just as well park in the street; she had trouble manoeuvering into the driveway anyway.

His head was pounding from the metallic glare of the highway as he backed up to the boat trailer and got out and hitched it to the Ford. The last time he had done this Duffy had been standing not three feet away from him, ready to help. They had lifted the heavy trailer together, he on one side and Duffy on the other, holding the white hitch so tightly that bits of white paint had flaked onto their palms from the metal.

Now he straddled the trailer, took the hitch in both hands and gave it a solid heave. He hadn't lined it up right. He hovered for a moment. The trailer was a fulcrum in his hands; he was an extension of the cold metal. It could rock him into the ground if his footing were not sure. With white knuckles he shifted the trailer an inch, centered it exactly above the hitch and brought it down slowly, fighting the metal with every breath. At last the trailer fit snugly into the hitch and he let go, breathed deeply, and watched the blood return to his hands. *Duffy, I'm strong enough for both of us, I'll win that goddam fifty bucks you didn't have to spend.* He completed the link-up with shaking hands. His hands still shook on the wheel of the Ford as he carefully hauled home the last catch Duffy would ever give him.

The minute he walked in, he knew somethng was wrong. The television was not on, and it was too early for Helen to start dinner. Usually he came in through the garage, but today he had left the car, with the trailer and boat hooked to it, in the driveway, behind Helen's Chevy, so he had come in through the front door. He stood in the foyer, listening. There were voices — Helen's and another woman — Mrs. Martin, be damned, the old crone in the corner house across from the lot where he burned his grass.

He started down the hall toward his bedroom, but Helen had heard him come in. She came out of the living room toward him.

"Carlyle, Mrs. Martin is here. About that burning. Don't you think you should talk to her?"

He paused and turned toward her. Her wispy gray hair was ' falling around her neck. She needed another permanent. She was probably going to spend her grocery money on it and then have to ask him for extra money next week. He did not look into her eyes.

"No, I don't want to talk to her. *You* talk to her. I got Duffy's boat out front. I'm gonna move your car out to the street."

He bit the words out hard and went on down the hall to his desk in the dining room. He could still hear them talking.

"But I *have* tried, Mrs. Simpson . . . I don't like calling the police, but if something isn't done . . . My linens, my draperies . . . If he could see the damage . . ."

She didn't have the guts to come over and yell at him. She was like Helen, nervous, scared. So she picked Helen to whine to. Two old idiots gabbling at each other. And that was just fine. Helen knew better than to try and get him in there again. Try closing the windows, she said, but Mrs. Martin *had* tried, the air-conditioning was so expensive . . . unbearably hot . . . He burned so *often* . . . couldn't take it any longer . . . have to take drastic measures . . .

He fished the extra set of keys to Helen's Chevy out of the drawer and went out through the garage entrance, not bothering to walk quietly. Helen was trying to steer Mrs. Martin toward the front door, speaking to her in that reassuring Cinderella voice she used to use with the children.

"I certainly will speak to him, I promise," she said.

He slammed the door behind him. Oh, she'd speak to him all right. As if she was the one could ever do the telling around this house. He stayed in the garage until the old bitch left and then went out to move Helen's car. He sat in it for a few minutes after he parked it, watching Mrs. Martin's tiny hunched back in its old dark dress hurrying back so she could hide behind windows and spy on the neighbors. When you thought about it, it was surprising that she had the guts to come over and complain. Of course she had only confronted Helen, not him. He felt some relief that Helen had kept her quiet. She would probably not come back again. It was a lot easier to hide in the house and call the police on the telephone. But *he* had no reason to hide. He left the Chevy and got into the Ford and backed it out of the driveway, turned slowly and then carefully backed the boat trailer into its new space in the other half of the garage. He braced the trailer with a couple of cinder blocks, unhitched it, and finally drove the Ford up next to it, leaving his car there next to Duffy's boat, where everybody could see it.

He stomped his shoes on the filthy, ragged grey mat in front of the door which separated the kitchen from the garage. Helen was scurrying around the kitchen, making dinner. Water was boiling in covered pots on the stove. He could hear the lids bubbling, and smell steam in the air. Potatoes, and he wasn't sure what else. He went into his bedroom and lay down in his dirty work pants and limp white shirt. His back had been good, even with all the running around, even lifting that boat trailer. He had been careful; it was like a bargain he had to keep. He tried not to do anything to antagonize his back and it didn't give him a lot of pain. Except sometimes even when he wasn't asking for it. Usually, though, he did something to it. The problem was he forgot, or if he didn't forget, he had to do things that had to be done and that would hurt his back. Like yesterday, carrying all those loads of dead grass. He was surprised that the trailer hadn't bothered him, but you couldn't assume anything with this back. The pain might catch him later in the evening. He tried to relax by looking through the crumpled up morning newspaper with the pillow wadded behind his head, and dozed off.

Helen had not told him Bob was coming to dinner. Carlyle had come to sit at the table and seen him, looking down at his plate. The table was set for three. Bob and Helen held the usual chitchat. They didn't really expect him to join in, although they knew he was listening. Bob had gotten a letter from Sarah. Helen thought Sarah might be depressed, being so far away, her first decent job in Washington. Carlyle was careful not to react in any way, but he was glad to hear Bob cut Helen off, refusing to indulge her senseless fears. Slowly he ate the rock cornish hen Helen had put in front of him. She and Bob shared one between them. It was one of Helen's better dishes. Too bad she didn't cook it more often. They left the table while he was still eating, and started clattering around in the kitchen. Later they went to watch television, without coming back to clear his place. he sat a moment, and lit a cigar.

It was not yet dark when he took his cigar to the back yard, watching the smoke rise before his eyes past the tops of the trees. He ignored the minister's overgrown mess next door and saw only the smooth green sheet of his own property, tucked up nice and even at the boundary by the row of Norfolk Island pine. You didn't see those everywhere in the Gulf coast area. They were some of the prettiest trees he knew. They added a kind of elegance to any place: tall, symmetrical, they took their time growing to the height of a three story house. Ten years ago he had planted them and they were only now coming into their finest growth. But they were trees worth waiting for. Helen had pointed them out once when they were driving the kids someplace. They had driven past a long driveway which was lined by closely set Norfolk Island and Australian pine. Helen admired the effect and when he retired he had planted these.

"They've really shot right up there, haven't they?"

Bob was standing there, upwind from the gray cigar smoke, with his hands in his pockets, his head down, keeping his distance. Carlyle nodded. Bob took after Helen. Even though the kid was tall — taller than Carlyle — and muscular, he was always fidgeting; a nervous weakling inside. He had let his hair grow too long: pale brown curls reached his shoulders or were pulled back into a ponytail, like tonight. He had Helen's blue-green eyes, and under that scraggly mess he had a good strong chin. It was painful to see a perfectly decent-looking man throwing his youth away, hiding it under a lot of hair. He had tried to tell him once, but of course he got nowhere. When Bob grew up and stopped hiding, he would probably find out his good looks were gone; he'd find out that he had shaved and cut his hair just when he was starting to look like the old man.

He spat some of the tobacco taste from his mouth and stood with his wrists crossed behind his back. He still held the slowly dying cigar.

"Mom says they had Mr. Mills' funeral yesterday."

Carlyle kept looking straight ahead, watching a squirrel running along the telephone wire that bordered the lot. It kept stopping and tilting his head to one side. What was it listening to? Humming in the wires, maybe, or leaves rustling? A soft breeze stirred the grass; it carried a faint salt smell from Bonita Bay. Carlyle closed his eyes. When he opened them again, the squirrel was gone. There was a commotion in the birdbath in the center of the yard.

"Damned bluejays!" he said. "Keep bothering the sparrows." He flicked the dead cigar onto the ground and crushed it automatically under his heel.

"That's a nice boat he left you."

"Get on outa there, you!" Carlyle shouted at the bluejay descending into a crowd of sparrows, scattering them all. "Ought to go get that .22 after him." But he didn't move.

"Sixteen-footer, right?"

He turned without answering and stepped through the grass which was damp with evening fog, around the corner of the garage, to the driveway. He slapped the boat's small hull and traced the identification numbers with his forefinger. FL 3495, A 21. He did not turn his head to see if Bob had followed him. Kid who had been busted for selling dope trying to egg up to the old man because now he wanted a job. Spent his time on his ass in the bedroom with the shades down listening to trash music. Hiding. If he did go out in the sun it would just be for a tan to get the girls. No, he did not particularly care whether Bob bothered to follow him to the boat.

The white paint was chipped in places; he felt for rust. Lower on the hull there were barnacles he would have to knock off. He stepped onto the trailer, just above the wheel and carefully leaned over the edge of the boat. All coated with sand and dust, the four blue vinyl seats, the plastic steering wheel cracked from the sun, the storage compartments . . . He felt the boat shake and looked up. Bob had joined him. Carlyle looked away again, focusing on the blue seats.

"Plan to take it out any time soon?"

The question was quiet, careful, the way Helen was careful. Bob's voice was soft, like Helen's. He had her blue-green eyes and breathy voice. Always wanting to read when he was a kid; he got that from Helen too. When she worked on the Hill she used to take the bus back into the city even on her days off so she could read at the Library of Congress. Bob might not have heard about that. It might be something he would like to know about his mother. Bob read too much when he was a kid; Carlyle had taken him out fishing a few times, trying to change that. Bob was still standing there patiently, waiting for him to say something, not looking at him. Was he thinking of those fishing trips fifteen years ago? His father taking him on the commercial deep sea excursions, bringing home huge grouper and once even a tarpon, cleaning a couple dozen fish on the workbench in the garage while the boy sat on a bucket and watched. Carlyle cleared his throat and spoke.

"Don't know when I'll get a chance now. I'm tied up with this damned house business, but I might try getting out one morning for a couple hours."

He knew Bob knew that the house was not a stupid business to him, but talking about it the way it really was would not be right either. It was something he had to carry inside himself for a while, where it wouldn't be ruined right away. He had to decide about

Scovill: he didn't want Rodney Scovill laying a hand on Beaumont's house, but Scovill was right when he said who else could he get now that Starritt wasn't working. So he would probably have to hire Scovill after all, and then hound him every inch of the way to make sure he didn't ruin it, and end up doing a lot of the work over again himself, which is what he always had to do when he hired bad people.

He didn't know what else to say to Bob, so he went on. "Yeah, that house will keep me busy. We poured the flooring. Going to be moving fast now."

Bob didn't answer, and what could he say, anyway? He wouldn't just come right out and ask for a job. He couldn't, because of all the years he had lived in this house and all that had happened between them. His son couldn't get or keep a decent job, he used to smoke dope and maybe he still did. Carlyle thought suddenly of the knife that had cut its way between them long before Bob wore his hair too long for a man.

It was a new fishknife, one of the better Christmas gifts from Helen. He had taken the boy out on his tenth birthday. It was a Sunday. He woke him at four a.m., loaded him with the tackle box and headed off in plenty of time to catch the deep sea boat. The boy had really liked it; he was so excited when he hauled in a big grouper that he dropped his rod and ran around the deck with it. The old fishermen had gotten a real kick out of him. They had come back to the garage that day with more than twenty grouper. He gave Bob the knife and told him to clean the fish he had caught so his mother could fix it for dinner.

The boy's face and arms were bright pink. The skin was going to blister and peel. Maybe he had kept him out too long, but he shouldn't have been so pale in the first place. He stayed indoors with his mother too much. But kids didn't know enough to stop when they liked something — sun, rain or candy . . . You had to judge for them, set an example when you thought about it.

He picked up the nine pound grouper and slapped it onto the newspaper covering the workbench. The fish wobbled for a minute. Its dead eye reminded him of the ugly black onyx ring his mother had left him. He had given it to Helen before they were married.

Bob stood with his knife poised above the fish, staring at its head. He was frowning and his throat jerked.

"You know the way. You been watching me long enough. Go on, start with the head. It's easy."

The boy raised the knife. His nail-bitten hand was trembling; the knuckles made a broken white stripe on his sunburned skin. He hesitated, looked at the fish. Carlyle tried to catch his eye and realized suddenly that his son was afraid of him. He must have looked like that, silent, terrified, many nights when Carlyle came home late for dinner and slammed the front door. He must stand, looking like this, at his bedside, not reading, listening, hearing every sound his father made, every word he said to his mother — and yes, of course, he heard the dishes crack against the wall, he heard Helen whimpering the week before when he twisted her arm behind her back and shoved her face close to the greasy kitchen sink. The boy had ears on him, didn't he, dammit!

Carlyle wrenched the knife from the pink hand, pushed the boy away from the bench and hacked off the fishhead.

"Go on in and clean yourself up. If you ain't ready to clean what you catch, you shouldn't expect to eat it either."

His son had stumbled backward toward the door. Carlyle knew that tone had come into his voice, the tone he hated himself but he couldn't seem to get rid of. Later Bob came to the table and sat without eating, although Carlyle was already sorry he had lost his temper, and would not have kept Bob from eating the fish. The boy had not even tasted the birthday cake Helen had baked for him; he told his mother he wasn't feeling well. Carlyle told Helen he thought Bob had had too much sun. He was grateful that Bob had not brought him into it.

He had not seen much of either of his children; both Bob and Sarah had hidden in their rooms at night — they probably hurried to finish dinner before his car door slammed, and they came out later after he had eaten and gone back to his bedroom. That was when they were older. To them, he was a stranger who was nasty to their mother. He could not tell them how he wished he was not the way he was: Helen seemed to bring out the worst in him. He never told them.

Now he and his son were two men, standing facing each other, balanced on the trailer. Bob wanted the job, he needed it, and Carlyle was going to have to hire ten just like him, it didn't matter who, the workers were just workers, so why not, why not? Why not just say right out now, just say straight out, *Come and work for me, son?* He cleared his throat and shifted his legs; the boat moved slightly.

"Reckon you know I'll be hiring some construction workers in the next couple weeks."

He waited.

It was hard. He tried again, forcing down the words that wanted to come up and ruin it, swallowing the bitter things that came so easily to the surface.

"I need good workers, and it isn't easy work. If you think you want to work harder for your old man that you've ever worked before, well . . ."

Bob's face clinched. He just stood there and said nothing.

"The floor's not settled yet. So come Wednesday early, and we'll find something for you to do. You know where the site is?"

Why couldn't he have said it different, why did he have to put that cutting edge on it? Well, so far he didn't know any different than that the boy *was* lazy. Why not leave that out, though, just once? He waited, but Bob still didn't say anything.

"Well," Carlyle said, finally, "you think it over. If you decide you want the job, report to the site early Wednesday."

He could leave it at that. Did the boy have another job in mind? Well, whatever it was, so long as he got himself some work.

He stepped off the trailer. A jagged pain tore across his back. This damp air hadn't helped. What did he expect, anyway, after all these years, that the kid would jump at the chance?

"So long, Pop," Bob called. He was going over to his junk car, to drive away. "Thanks for the offer. I'll think about it."

If Bob had learned to be a good carpenter, he wouldn't have this Scovill problem. Funny how all of a sudden he wanted Bob to work for him and he didn't want Scovill. His back shot arrows up his spine at every step as he walked slowly into the house to look up Mr. Rodney Scovill's telephone number. He would probably have to hire the Scovill kid, too, even if all he had learned was how to plane doors.

The next morning he woke even before Helen was up. He couldn't fall asleep again. He lay in bed, waiting for the sun to rise, listening to the bugs crackling in his screens, the big fat palmetto bugs that ran back and forth along the window sills outside, disappearing before light came behind the shutters and into the plants. They only came out in the dark, and they thrived in this humid climate near the bay. Sometimes they got into Helen's kitchen. They wouldn't go anywhere that was clean; if she'd keep the kitchen clean, not a single bug would ever show up there. If you left food out they found it. But only if you left it out, and it was Helen's fault that they had gotten into the house. The light finally came, and he did not hear the bugs any longer; he did not want to dirty up his day thinking about them. He wanted to get to the site, to see if the flooring was settled yet.

He arrived just after sunrise, not the best time to check, but if it was ready he would know. He walked across the lot to where the stakes and foundation outlined the house that was to come. He bent down slowly and scanned the surface critically for lumps or flaws of any kind — a crease, a simple line, even the tiniest crack could mean trouble — and he wouldn't stand for it. He looked carefully, concentrating his vision, and found nothing wrong. He used the level, walking to all sides and using it again and again. Finally he put down the level and decided to rely on his eyes; they were all he had to go on. When it came to choosing the right shades of paint for the interior only his eye could do it — no instructions — and he trusted his eye, not the level, to test the flooring. His eye was a gift, like intuition or common sense. His judgment told him the floor was solid; he would never trust another man to tell him that.

He bent to examine the surface one last time and again found nothing. Gradually he straightened to his full height. He felt no pain, only a sense of wonder he had not felt for ten years, in all the time he had been retired. Here was the house begun, and he knew in the only way he could count on that it had been begun right. Day by day he would come and, step by step, check with his own senses for flaws in the work. The early morning air was cool; he inhaled deeply and exhaled, tasting the air. He allowed himself a tinge of tentative affirmation and gave a nod to the foundation laid.

THREE

RAIN
AND CLUTTER

Two weeks into construction and he was damn near close to schedule, reasonably satisfied with the work to date. Yesterday the site had begun to look like a house, with enough of the outer structure completed to make him say to Bob, "It's looking all right, isn't it? All right." Bob wasn't saying much, but he did his work and so far Carlyle had no complaints. Yesterday they had all put in a full day. He had gone to bed early, more relaxed than he had been in days, looking forward to a good night's rest. He had no dreams.

Waking to a steady humming long before light had come, he had instinctively drawn the sheet and the chenille bedspread over his chest, sensing a wet chill. In warm weather he always slept with the windows and the glass door to his bedroom open. The wet air had come into the room. He reached out and touched the nightstand, feeling the slightest moisture: hardly there, but undeniable. Reluctantly, he rose from the bed to close the windows. Helen was snoring in the other room, it would not be long before she woke, feeling the chill before she heard the quiet rain. Years ago, Helen had liked to sleep when it rained. The summer she was pregnant with Bob she had slept nearly every afternoon during the thundershowers. Sometimes when he came home early he would watch her curled up asleep like a child, with one knee against her growing belly.

He rotated the handle of the jalousies; gradually they fell flush with the house, covered with the smooth layers of rain. He stood at the open glass door of the porch, shivering slightly in the fine, misty air, which was rich with the smell of earth and rain. Outside was sheer blackness; the morning would be cloudy. Gratefully, he went back to bed.

When he woke again, his arms were cold outside the sheet; it was still raining. The digital alarm clock Helen had given him last Christmas (he never set the alarm) said that it was already nine-thirty, although the room was still dark. *Late.* He lay still. The rain was going to continue without letting up, so no work could be done at the site. The roof wasn't up yet. He looked through the glass door to the porch. A cloudy morning and if it were a light drizzle he would be at the site now, but with this kind of rain no one would even bother showing up. A day lost, and nothing he could do about it.

He got up and took his winter bathrobe from the closet; he was cold. He went to the kitchen, found the newspaper where Helen had left it on the table and took it back to the bedroom. In a few minutes she was hovering in the doorway, not venturing into the bedroom.

"You be ready for breakfast in a minute?"

Just like Sunday, when he usually slept late, and sometimes didn't want breakfast. So she usually asked him, or didn't bother at all.

"Yeah, I guess so. Just one egg. Poached."

"All right. It'll be ready in a minute, and the coffee's on, too."

So don't take too long coming out and let it get cold. As if it was his fault that the food was bad. She would never say it, but he could hear the slight tension in her voice. "And the coffee's on too." The "too" was almost a plea.

In the middle of breakfast the wall phone rang. Helen got up from the table and answered it.

"Pete Sanders," she said, as he came to take the phone. "Long distance."

He had to listen to Sanders' garbage first: how are you, Carlyle, too long since we've seen you, Mavis sends her regards to Helen, all the things people said before they came out and told you what they really wanted. When he finally got around to it, what Sanders wanted was to buy the acreage in North Carolina that Carlyle had been holding onto for years. It was good property, with excellent drainage and lots of trees. Carlyle had built a cabin there when he had lived near Asheville as a young man. He and Helen had spent their honeymoon there. Then later there were a few summers when he had driven the three of them to Carolina to visit the family, and he had gone back to see the land again. Now here Sanders was, calling long distance, saying he wanted to buy it.

"Okay, Pete, I'll think about it. Let me give you a call in a few days, huh?"

"Sure, Carlyle. Only don't keep me waiting too long."

After breakfast Helen followed him to the garage.

"If you're not going to work today, do you think you could see about that table?"

He thought a minute. What the hell.

"Yeah. Guess I might as well look at it."

He would not begrudge her the fixing of it, if he could get to it through all the clutter she had managed to pile up in the garage. She had filled the house with antiques and they had overflowed into the garage. Long ago he had told her not to have all this stuff shipped down from her mother's house in Carolina; he told her that the wood would warp and rot in this humidity. But she had it shipped anyway, and paid for it herself, out of a legacy from her aunt. And then a month ago her friend Elaine had brought down this drop-leaf oak dining room table.

"I don't know how you expect me to get to it with all this junk you got piled up in front of it. Gonna have to move all this *shit* first."

Something moved across Helen's face, like a shadow; she made a short clucking noise with her tongue.

"All *right*," he said. "Well, you take that end of this loveseat and let's move it over to that other wall."

She got a grip underneath the piece and he took the other end, careful to keep it lower than hers, keeping his eye on her spindly legs. She had broken her ankle once helping him lift a piece of furniture. He couldn't afford to let that happen again. Cost over a hundred bucks. She backed slowly toward the opposite wall, breathing hard. When she was ready to put it down, she looked at him, managed to exhale "Okay," and gently lowered her end of it.

"Don't know what you're keeping all this junk for in the first place. More in the house than you'll ever use and all this stuff out here just rotting away."

"You know I'm keeping these things for Sarah. They're not in your way, so I don't see why you have to be so nasty about it anyway." She spoke almost automatically as if she were tired of

saying the words. She took the arm of a rocker, tried to lift it and
rocked it over her big toe, poking out of open-toed flat sandals. He
winced. She bit her lip.

"Dammit, you shouldn't be trying to lift that anyway. Just get on
outa here and I'll get to the damn table myself, if it isn't already
ruined."

But she got another grip on the rocker and dragged it to the wall,
stubbornly ignoring him and refusing to make a sound. He knew
that if he hadn't been there she would have yelled and maybe said,
"Damnation!" when she hurt her toe. He had heard her before
when she thought she was alone. It was just her stubbornness that
she wouldn't say it in front of him.

She did leave then, because she knew he was going to get to her
damned table, whether she helped or not. He preferred not having
her around. Even when she tried to help, having her there meant
trouble.

He fought his way to the table at last, wondering how Helen and
Elaine had ever gotten it in there with all that other stuff around it.
He lifted the cane-backed chairs from the top of it, one at a time,
and set each of them down. After he had set down the last chair onto
the concrete floor, he paused to survey the drop-leaf.

Even as an antique, it wasn't worth much. The surface was
nicked and stained, probably with burn marks. It needed to be
completely refinished. Why anyone would want to treat a perfectly
good oak table that way was something he could not understand.
But he supposed that made as much sense as Helen hanging on to
all this junk, for sentimental reasons, so she could leave them to the
children. She had always been like that, confusing her family with
the pieces of junk they gave her. Must have packed up seventeen
boxes full of crystal serving platters after the wedding. To his recol-
lection she had never used more than one. But all seventeen boxes
were taking up space in her cabinets, you could be sure of that. Like
all those ugly nightgowns her mother had given her to take on the
honeymoon, she had worn one because she got cold when it rained.

It was the rain he remembered, rain that did not stop for a week,
that kept them in the cabin and the bed. Here in the garage the
concrete floor sent up a thick, musty odor, like the smell of wet

sidewalks. Back in that cabin the room had been filled with the smell of sex, and when they opened the window a fresh, clean smell came in, making Helen shiver and run her delicate fingers up and down her slender arms, under the white sleeves of her nightgown, designed only for some foolishness, some primness, not for comfort or warmth. Sex had been best during the heaviest downpours, when Helen, a little frightened, though not admitting it, of the thunder and the bright lightning, would open to him, her arms clasping him to her urgently, as if she was afraid of losing him in all the noise. And she never made a sound.

She had kept wanting to wash her hair, and he wouldn't let her, because he could not bear having to wait for it to dry. He liked to have it near him, where he could smell the richness of it, thick, rich hair darker than his own. Even when it was dirty, it did not lose that wonderful, feminine smell; even later, when the wedding permanent began to grow out, his hands still shook whenever he touched it, and for many years after the honeymoon, the thought of any other man ever smelling the scent of Helen's hair was enough to send him into a rage.

She often said no man ever had, ever would, how could he think such a thing. And if he wasn't drunk, he believed her. When he had enough whiskey in him, sometimes it seemed he saw something she didn't want him to see, and then he was no longer certain. So he had not believed her then and had left her crying afterwards.

He sanded the table, wanting to strip it back to where the good, clean smell of honest wood could come through. It would take days of work. He would not mind it so much if the table was worth something, but it was just an ordinary table, and it would cost more to have it moved to Washington than to buy a new one. It was just plain foolish, this hanging onto things that were worthless. Duffy's boat was different; it was something that could be used. It wasn't as if he already had a boat. Helen and Sarah had their own dining room tables (whatever Sarah had in that apartment served the purpose, he was sure) and keeping an extra table around that couldn't be used, or wouldn't be used, probably for years — if ever — just didn't make sense. Much of what Helen did simply made no sense. She had been to college but she could drive him to rage when she failed to see the simple sense about things. Like the way she treated Bob and Sarah, even though they were grown — always wanting to hang onto them, not able to let them go. Maybe Helen kept all this stuff to make up for all the people she couldn't keep. One of these days he would go in there and empty out all her closets and throw out all the clutter, all the useless junk. See whether or not it actually would kill her not to have all that shit around.

The rain did not let up. He thought of the acreage in Carolina, where the lot was covered with trees. Strong undergrowth it would take a tractor to cut through. The lot would have to be cleared if Sanders wanted to build there. Still, it was worth more than five thousand an acre.

Helen came out of the house, wearing a raincoat and a plastic rain hat, carrying her black pocketbook. She had put on a pair of black shoes, shiny patent leather.

"Thought I'd get some oysters, for oyster stew. Would you like some for lunch?"

He did not stop sanding to look her in the eye. He didn't like to be asked about food hours before the meal. It was only ten o'clock.

"Anything. I could eat a sandwich or something. Yeah, oyster stew sounds all right."

She walked out into the rain, her purse in one hand, holding the chinstraps on the rainhat with the other, her shoes clicking on the driveway. He watched her walk past Duffy's boat and down to her car in the street. She opened the door, quickly sat inside, and pulled it shut, hard. Before fumbling with her keys, she fiddled with the rain hat and looked in the mirror.

There was a bad nick in the table's surface. He worked hard to it for a while, but it wouldn't smooth out. Sanding would not be enough. He did not think anything could remove it. He stepped back to rest, and wiped the sweat from his face and arms with his handkerchief. But his skin still felt wet. Rain like this made the garage and house like steam rooms. As the day wore on, it would get worse, and he would feel dirty with the kind of sweat that does not evaporate, but soaks back into the skin. He hated the feeling of not being able to get sweat off his skin, and it made the garage, with its cinderblock walls and dull concrete floor, seem like a cell with an open end. He was tempted to quit, leave the table for later, and go to Johnny's, where the air-conditioning would chill away the sweat and wake him from this humid sluggishness. But there was no sense going out in weather like this just to waste time somewhere.

Helen hated to drive in the rain almost as much as she hated to drive at night. It seemed she had to go somewhere every day, even if it was only to the grocery store, even in weather like this. She never drove far and never stayed out long. She always changed her dress and shoes. That was something he couldn't understand. Still, on a rainy day like this, there would be women in the stores with curlers in their hair under their scarves and, ridiculous as the plastic lavender rain hat looked, Helen would not be one of those women. She never wore curlers in her hair, and she did not own a single pair of pants. So many women crammed their overweight bodies into ugly doubleknit slacks. Helen had never pulled that one yet, and he was certain she never would.

It was too quiet. He had not heard the sound of an engine. He turned and looked at her car, still in the street. Helen was sitting there, her hands gripping the top of the steering wheel. She raised her right hand above the wheel and grimaced. She hesitated, and then let her right hand, limp, open, fall to the wheel.

She got out of the car and walked back up the driveway, nervous; he could tell by the way she avoided looking at him, keeping her eyes down, her hands in her coat pockets. The rain hat had slipped back on her head and her loose grey curls poked out, getting wet.

She stood inside the garage, waiting.

"My car won't start. I think the battery may be dead."

"Don't see any reason why it should be."

She shook her head slightly and said nothing, still holding the keys in one hand, the purse in the other. She stood a moment longer, looking tired, as if she had just been through a major struggle and didn't have any energy left over.

There was no good reason why she should be so upset. She could just as well go to the store tomorrow, when it might not be raining. But she *had* put on a girdle and a decent dress, and even good stockings with no runs. She dressed as she always dressed to go to the grocery store or to church. He could not remember when she had begun to buy the ugly housedresses, the cheap summer shifts she never wore outside. Maybe she had always been like that, perhaps it was only an illusion he had had once, that she had dressed for him.

She had begun to walk past him when he thrust out his arm.

"Give me the keys."

She paused, and he took them quickly. She went back into the house, probably to work on her knitting.

He found his hat and the battery tester and went out into the rain. The battery was dead. Maybe the alternator had failed. He could not believe the battery was three years old; he remembered so clearly when he had bought it. By the time he returned to the garage, his shirt was soaked. He took it off and laid it on the washing machine.

Helen was in the family room, wearing a bathrobe and slippers, knitting on some kind of multicolored afghan, mostly brown and orange. The colors Sarah liked. Earth tones. Warm colors. He could imagine Sarah, alone in her tiny apartment, finding the Washington winter too cold, but refusing to admit it. Helen would suffer with the afghan on her lap all summer, just to have it ready for Sarah before Christmas. He watched her hands clicking the needles in steady rhythm, back and forth, crossing over again and again, tiny stitch by tiny stitch. She wore thick glasses to see the tiny loops. Her hands had remained slender, the purplish veins standing out on her pale, wrinkled skin.

When she looked up, he caught her eyes for just a second before they glanced down at his bare chest and then away.

"Well, the battery's dead," he told her. "Ever notice whether the needle on your gauge moves to the 'C' or not?"

She put down her knitting, and a skein of orange yarn rolled across the floor toward the television set.

"You mean when I start the car?" She raised her hand to her lips, a gesture he was glad to see. She would think about the question objectively, not hysterically. Warm and settled in her bathrobe, with her knitting on her lap, Helen did have the ability not to be hysterical.

"I'm not sure," she said. "I *think* it's been moving to the 'C' right when I start the car, but I can't remember *lately* if it has or not. Maybe not, lately. I'm not sure. Do you think the alternator has gone out?"

He wasn't surprised she knew the word, although he would lay down money she didn't know what an alternator was. Helen could pick up words she had heard him use about a car, and never bother to figure out how the thing worked. Then she could put her finger to her lips and look like somebody seriously thinking about something important, and use the word. It seemed to give her pleasure, and probably it didn't do any real harm. Still, there was something about it he didn't like.

"Might be. I dunno. I'll have to jump it to find out."

She sat perfectly still, one hand clutching her knitting, the other pressed against her cheek. Waiting.

"Well, it's raining pretty hard out there," he said. "Do you have to go anywhere today?"

She dropped her hand to her lap.

"Oh, well, not really, I suppose."

Don't you dare start whining and sighing, he thought. Suddenly blood rushed to his head. He drew his lips together tight and folded his arms across his bare chest, the deep tan of his forearms making a stripe he could see when he looked down at his white belly.

They waited like that in silence, and he sensed there was something she wanted to say, but wouldn't unless he spoke first. He knew there was plenty of food in the refrigerator, or they could just as well eat canned soup from the pantry.

"You had some place besides the store to go to?"

She wouldn't look at him, and started knitting again, counting her stitches carefully, moving her lips silently. She would wait until he left the room before she went to pick up the skein of yarn on the floor; she seemed to dislike doing any housework in front of him.

"Don't you think you should put on a shirt? You might catch cold, even standing in here, with that draft from the garage."

He felt comfortable without his shirt; he was not cold, even though the house was less steamy than the garage. Helen had some place to go she didn't want to tell him. Probably to visit a girlfriend or to the church. They were planning a bazaar soon, and Helen was always involved with those things. Time and money. He knew those church people didn't like him much, and he knew she wouldn't give up doing things for the church, but so long as she didn't make him listen to stories about any of it, he was willing to let it go. An unspoken agreement. If she really needed to go somewhere, she could ask him to take her. But he wasn't about to take her to any damned church meeting on a day like this.

He left the room, stepping over the skein of yarn, and went back to his bedroom. He put on a clean sportshirt, and stood before the glass door to the porch, watching the rain swell suddenly to a downpour.

Two days straight it rained, breaking at times only to leave a heavy mist in the air, periods of silence with only an occasional birdsong. It was a false silence, because when he stopped sanding and strained to listen, he heard the faint dripping of water running downward, leaf to leaf, in the foliage. He could hear it in the crotons he had planted along the garage wall for color. He finally finished the sanding on the third day and left the garage, not wanting to stay in the house, but unable to think of anywhere he wanted to go.

Like a prison. Like a goddamned prison, and he hated it. Caught him full in the teeth. He stood in the porch, folded his arms across his chest and stared helplessly at the rain pouring down the screens. Sheer transparent sheets of it, gushing out of control. The soil was already soggy as sponge and his schedule was off. Nothing to do but wait it out, and he hated few things as passionately as he hated to wait. He hated standing by and watching anyone, except maybe a good game of football or a wrestling match.

For the past few days he had not felt like wrestling, and probably would not want to wrestle for a few more. Sanding the table had left his muscles sore. He would leave it like that, freshly sanded and unstained. See how Sarah liked it next time she came to visit. Maybe he would tell her how much he had hated doing it and would not have done it at all except that he was trapped by the damned rain for three days straight.

He was ready for a beer, but he did not want to go to Johnny's.

Rain like this always put him into a black mood if it kept on long enough. He didn't like going to the place when he was not in the mood to wrestle or joke. Helen knew he was in one of his moods, and had stayed out of the garage except to announce meals. She had not said anything more to him than she had to, and the quiet had allowed him to remain calm. Several times when he had walked past her in the family room, or had sat across from her at the table, he had not been able to keep from wondering if she remembered the cabin and the rain in North Carolina. He was sure she did. He was sure she remembered the way they seemed to share the rain, shut off in their own small place together, surrounded by the noise of the hard, steady downpour. Yesterday, at lunch, as he lifted his soup spoon, he had seen her looking past him out the window, at the rain. Just from the way her two hands were wrapped around her teacup, as if she were ill and clutching at nourishment, just from this, he knew, he was certain, she remembered too. Helen, do you remember the rain? He almost said it out loud.

But talking about it would ruin it. He would always remember it the way he knew it was, the way she had let him, her first man, warm her shivering, delicate body with a warmth only he could give her, and how in turn she had given him something, something he could not name but which he needed too. He had needed Helen then, and he had let her cradle his head in her arms while he slept like a child. Maybe they had known even then, how bit by bit, inch by inch, the ground would slip from under them.

Bob's car pulled into the driveway, he did not ask where she was going with Bob. When the car pulled up again, two hours later, he did not ask where she had been besides the grocery store. If she wanted him to know, she would tell him. And if she had needed him to take her, she would have asked him, although he knew she still held it against him that he had broken his word to her a few times. The last time her car was on the blink he was supposed to be back in time to take her to a doctor's appointment, and he had forgotten. When he looked at the clock in Johnny's, he saw he was already half an hour late, so he had not bothered to go home at all. He hated to take her places where she would spend money, and doctors always wanted a lot of money for nothing.

At least he had asked Bob to help him jump her car. The alternator was fine. It was hard to believe that three years had passed since he bought the last battery, but when he found the warranty in his desk, the date was expired. Bob had asked when he thought they would go back to work, Carlyle shrugged his shoulders and said, Whenever it clears up.

The birds came to the feeders despite the rain. They ate and shook the water from their wings, and flew back up to the telephone wires. The grass was already an inch higher than he liked to see it. After this rain it would be tough to mow. Thicker, longer, and still wet, it would resist the blades and fill up the carrier twice as quickly. But it would be healthier and richer.

Helen came to the porch.

"I've got hot soup ready."

He turned to look at her, her words already an echo, recurring in layer upon past layer of the same words uttered in the same voice years ago. He knew what kind of soup. Vegetable beef.

She had set the table nicely, with the pale linen luncheon tablecloth, a wedding gift from somebody in her family. Even though it was marred by grease stains, it still didn't look too bad. It was a change from the usual placemats on the bare table.

Helen shivered as she sat down, drawing her dingy, stretched-out grey sweater close around her drooping shoulders. Her arthritis bothered her when it rained this long.

Although he was not hungry, he ate, spooning the hot soup slowly, trying to enjoy it. Helen was not eating. The aspirin she took for the arthritis upset her stomach. She had taken the trouble to make the homemade soup, had laid the tablecloth, for him. Although he could not enjoy the soup, he did not dislike it, either, and would just as soon eat it as not.

"On the news they predicted three more days of rain. That hurricane could still come here," Helen said.

"Must be running out of steam by now."

Helen was fascinated with hurricanes and other natural disasters. Every day she mentioned the newest storm she had watched on the radar they used on the six o'clock news.

"They said it's growing stronger, since it changed its course."

"Could change again." He said it because he hoped it would. If a hurricane came through, it would mean more waiting. He put down his soup spoon. "If it keeps on like this I might just take that trip on up to Carolina, get that property taken care of." He hadn't thought he would, until he said so, but suddenly it seemed right. Get away from this waiting.

"You mean the place Sanders wants?"

He could not be certain, but her tone seemed calm, not hysterical, as he might have expected.

"Yeah. Thought I'd go ahead and sell it to him. We could invest in something down here, or get some bonds. I'm tired of worryin' with that place."

It was time to let that property go. He had been putting it off, but suddenly his mind seemed fixed, resolved on the action, and he felt relieved.

Helen stood up and began clearing away the dishes, her baggy grey sweater and dingy apron strings hanging down her back. He followed her into the kitchen and stood rubbing his chin. She set the dishes down on the counter and turned on the water.

"Yeah. I want to get rid of that place. Guess I'll call Saunders and leave in the morning." He would have to go out and buy a new battery for Helen's car, but then he could just leave. Drive in the rain, be out of Georgia by midnight, maybe, and into Carolina the next afternoon. The water was running and he couldn't be sure that she answered him. The dishes clacked as she slipped them into the filling sink.

FOUR

SELLING
THE LAND

He drove ten miles faster than the posted limit, determined to clear the Florida line by dark. He had been waiting at the shopping mall at nine o'clock that morning, holding the dead battery and getting soaked. When the doors opened, he was the first customer. He got the new battery, put it in Helen's car, packed a suitcase and was on his way by ten-thirty.

He could not remember how many times he had made this trip. It always seemed to be in the summertime, and he always left before first light, sometimes rising at three a.m. and waking the children, who rubbed their eyes and carried their pillows to the car. This morning Helen had been awake early, and had made sure he took the foil-wrapped pound cakes and apricot bread — three packages for him and two to give to the Sanders. "You'll be close enough to go ahead and see Sarah," Helen had said. But Washington was almost another day's drive; he didn't have the time. Sarah would be home at Christmas anyway.

By the time he reached northern Florida he had driven past the rain. The sun beat down, and the small water drops vanished from the hood and windshield. He pulled off at an exit to buy gasoline, and when he came back to the interstate he noticed a hitchhiker. Never could tell what they might be carrying. Might look like a harmless kid and then turn on you with a knife or a gun.

Already his back was stiff. He would have to be careful not to drive too far. If he pushed even so much as an extra half hour, he would pay for it for days. Perhaps there was no way to get out of some pain, this trip. He would try to make it at least to Forsyth, stay at that motel with the nice old couple who always remembered him and asked about Florida. What was the name? He couldn't remember. He usually stayed there on his way back. Going up he had always driven a few hours more, and didn't have to stay overnight. Coming back, he would leave later in the day. With the late start he had made today, he would have to be satisfied to reach Forsyth.

There was a restaurant in Lake City where he used to stop for late breakfasts on other trips; it would be long past lunchtime when he passed that exit today, and he would not bother to stop. The pound cake would keep him until dinner. He unwrapped one of the loaves with his right hand, steering with his left. He broke off a chunk of the cake, and took a big bite.

The country was pretty up here, no question about it. From Ocala on north, the land just kept rolling out, as if it was put there for one purpose and one purpose only: so that you could see the way the green meadows, cow pastures, and tree-covered hills looked at exactly that moment you drove past them. Of course it was foolish to think of it that way, but it was all right so long as it was just a thought.

By the time he passed Valdosta he was hot, tired and stiff and he thought he had better pull off the highway at one of the many exits between Valdosta and Macon. He was hungry; all the pound cake had done was make his mouth feel mushy. Bad for the teeth. He wanted something solid and not sweet. A good steak, maybe. He drove past a large new cafeteria and stopped at a small restaurant that might not be too crowded. He struggled out of his seat, feeling his back lock into a new stiffness, a knot that wouldn't pull apart.

Inside it was air-conditioned and cool. He washed in the men's room and made sure his hair was combed and his shirt was buttoned. A young hostess, wearing what looked like a nurse's white polyester uniform, showed him to a table. He ordered a steak dinner. The restaurant was not crowded; that was good. He liked to get in and out of restaurants quickly. Two tables over the waitress was serving a black family, a couple with two small children. It was just like television. Everywhere you go. Bob and Sarah had called him a racist when he said he wasn't going to sit there and watch that program with niggers in it. Well, if racist was what he was, that was what he was. Anytime he said something like that when one kid was in the room, whatever kid it was would get up and walk out, boiling mad and afraid to say anything. Then he would smile to himself. No way he was going to watch that garbage on television. Nothing you could do about restaurants and other places, but you didn't have to have them in your home.

The waitress came with his steak. Her broad smile irritated him. *Is that the same smile you gave them, miss? I want a different one.* The steak was tough and tasteless. Hard to chew. Two young men were talking at the table behind him.

"All you have to do is accept Him as your Savior," one of them said in a flat, calm voice. "That's all you have to do." Carlyle had heard religious people speaking in that voice before. It made him uneasy; he felt as though he were listening to a zombie. Helen still went to church; he had stopped going years before. He always fell asleep there anyway. He told Helen it was because his daddy had made him go on Wednesdays and twice on Sundays and sing in the choir too. So he smiled when he heard the other young man's voice answering; this one was savvy and cool.

"Oh, yeah, right. Listen, man, it was good talking to you. Thanks for the coffee. But I got to go now."

He watched the guy walk out the door. Long hair—nowhere as long as Bob's, but long enough—denim jacket and jeans. When you got down to it, he didn't know which was worse—religious zombies or longhairs. He gulped down his iced tea, left the waitress a small tip (the food was bad and he didn't like her smile), and paid his bill.

Outside the longhair in jeans came toward him.

"Hey, good sir, can you spare a quarter?"

The guy was just a lazy bum. He was surprised to see a clean, smooth-shaven face, clear blue eyes and a pleasant, white even-toothed smile. But there, hanging from the man's left earlobe, was a small gold hoop.

He averted his eyes and went directly to his car. He would not let himself think about it. He would not. Man with a damned earring! He just didn't know. He just didn't know.

It was not quite dark yet, but his back would not tolerate much more driving. He went another twenty miles to a Days Inn. He was annoyed that he could go no further. He would get to Pete's easily the next day, but he had not made it today even as far as Macon, let alone Forsyth, just the other side.

He drove into the Sanders driveway before dinnertime the next day. Pete and Mavis greeted him with as much warmth as they could muster under the circumstances: Billy, their only child, had run away from home: it seemed to Carlyle that the intensity of their concern bordered on hysteria. He suggested that he go to a motel, but they insisted he stay with them. He gave Mavis Helen's pound cake and apricot bread and offered what consolation he could.

"Listen, I ran away myself when I was a kid. The old man tanned me good the first time. The second time he just kicked me out for good."

After all, he said, Billy was sixteen, certainly old enough to survive in the world. But Pete wanted to go out and look for him. Carlyle said maybe it was time Billy got out there and found out what it was all about. It wouldn't kill him to miss a few meals.

"It's just that Mavis is so worried," Pete whispered, while Mavis was in the kitchen. But Pete was worried too. He sat and listened sympathetically to Mavis's ravings: Billy could get mixed up with the wrong kind of girl, he could be lost and cold and dirty, he could be kidnapped—wild fantasies from an overworked imagination. Pete was going to look for Billy, and when it came to deciding whether he should stay with Mavis or go with Pete, Carlyle went with Pete. He wasn't going to sit around saying, "Well, but Mavis . . ." and "Now, Mavis, that's just silly."

The first place Pete went to was a refuge in their suburban area where kids went to be babied. Carlyle would have preferred to wait in the car, but Pete looked at him, so he got out and went up the path with him. He hesitated at the bottom of the steps while Pete rang the doorbell. Who would open the door—some middle-aged lush with dyed red hair or a dirty blonde smoking a cigarette? Pete rang again, and then knocked. His shoulders had grown droopy since Carlyle had seen him last. His olive green sport coat hung awkwardly loose, creased around the hem. They could hear rock music playing inside.

After the third knock someone turned the music down; a face appeared behind a window curtain. Finally the door opened, and a teenaged boy eyed Pete suspiciously.

"Yeah? What d'you want?"

"I, uh, I'm looking for my son. Billy. Is he here? Or have you seen him?"

"Billy? I don't know any Billy. Ain't here, I guess."

"Yes, you *do* know Billy, and don't try and tell me any different. What are you playing games for? I just want to talk to him, for God's sake."

Pete had raised his voice; the timbre made Carlyle wince. A man who did not have the courage to raise his voice to his own son was not going to intimidate a stranger. The effect of this outburst on the kid in the doorway was predictable: his lips barely moved in his stony face as he looked at Pete and said softly, "He ain't here." He closed the door. After a moment the music was turned up again, so loud the wooden steps shook.

They walked back to the car in silence.

"I just don't understand," Pete said. "I don't see why they have to be so goddam *hostile*."

"You're letting this thing get to you, Pete. Why don't you just relax and he'll probably turn up before you know it."

Pete said staring straight ahead, his hands resting on the steering wheel, "I just don't know. You give them everything. I just can't figure it out."

When Pete finally started the car, Carlyle nursed his sore back and hoped it wouldn't be too long before he could lie down on a nice firm bed.

After a while Pete glanced at him.

"So you wouldn't do anything if it happened to you, Carlyle?"

Well, sure as hell. If Bob had ever run away, Carlyle would do the same thing his daddy had done when he ran away and he'd already told Pete what that was.

"I think you should just let it go. Let him learn for himself. He'll be back if he can't make it."

"But wouldn't you *miss* him? Wouldn't you worry?"

He was beginning to feel very embarrassed for Pete. And after all, no man had the right to tell another man how he should raise his son. He was relieved when they turned into Waterford Road, but then Pete drove right past the house.

"Don't know why I didn't think of it before. I'll talk to Jim — he's one of Billy's buddies. He's a nice kid. I can trust him. He worked for me last summer."

If he really wanted to get away, Carlyle thought, he wouldn't tell
his friend where he was going. He let Pete go up to the house alone
this time. Probably the family was eating dinner. The mother came
to the door after a while, and Pete went inside.

He was gone quite a while, and his shoulders dropped more
than ever when he came out.

"He doesn't know," he said. "He said Billy talked a lot about
California; he wrote a paper about San Francisco for school. He
thought maybe he might try to go there." Carlyle didn't say anything. "I guess we'd better check with Mavis," Pete said.

They sat in the living room, on Mavis's blue velvet couch. The
three of them, like a bunch of dumb monkeys, Carlyle thought
gloomily. He was tired and he ached.

"I don't understand," Pete said for the thousandth time. "He
never mentioned being upset, never acted like anything was wrong.
I could see if we'd had a fight or punished him for something. But to
disappear, just like that!" He tried to snap his fingers, but it didn't
come off.

After a silence, Pete got up suddenly. "This is no way to be
treating our guest, I guess, Mavis. How about if I fix some drinks."

With a bourbon in his hand, Carlyle found the Sanderses less
exasperating. Pete took his drink over to the fireplace and stood
there, leaning against the mantel.

"So what about that land, Carlyle?"

Carlyle stared into his glass. "Well, I been thinking about it.
Thought I'd go look at it again tomorrow. Let you know what I think
then."

"It's a pretty lot. I can see where you might not want to sell it.
But it doesn't look like you and Helen are going to be taking advantage of it. It's a shame."

It was true. They hadn't used the cabin in years, and they had
never got around to building a summer cottage there. Whenever
they visited up here they always stayed somewhere else — Helen
with her sister or brother; he with the Sanderses or other friends
from the old country club.

"Unless you're holding it for the kids," Pete said. "But I guess
Bob or Sarah, either one, don't plan to come here, do they?"

"We'll have to call the police if he isn't back by morning," Mavis said. "But maybe he'll call us." She seemed more relaxed than before, almost dreamy.

"The thing is," Pete said, and Carlyle groaned inwardly. They were going to start talking about Billy again.

He was roused out of a reverie to realize that Mavis was talking to him.

"Did you say Helen's eyesight is worse? Can she still drive?"

That's what they always asked. Not, Can she see? Never, Can she see to keep her house clean or to cook food without ruining it? It was always, Can she drive her damn car. She had learned to drive at the age of fifty-two, and now that was all her friends seemed to care about. She had survived for fifty-two years without knowing how to drive and she'd probably survive a good thirty more without driving if her sight got worse and it came to that.

"Yeah, she still drives. The grocery store, the church. Helen don't have reason to drive much." He knew what Mavis was thinking: *She needs to drive to get away from you, Carlyle*. He always wondered just how much Mavis knew. He was certain Helen never talked about things, but Mavis was nosy. It had been a good idea to move to Florida; there were too many people like Mavis here in Carolina, people whose families had been here so long that they thought they were better than everyone else. Carlyle's family went back a hundred years in Carolina, but that had never mattered to him. He had made his own life the way he wanted it, and he didn't care if nobody knew who he was or where he came from. Helen's family went back further, and they were like Mavis's people, always acting as if it was important who their grandfathers were. And that didn't prove a damn thing: a man was still trash if he didn't work to make something of himself. Helen had too many friends and too much family here. He was glad he had gotten away from all of it, from her family and her friends, all those people who thought they were something and never did anything worth a damn.

"It's been so long since I've seen Helen," Mavis said. "When are you going to bring her up here, Carly?" She pointed her face at him as if she was a wind-up doll; her rouged cheeks and red razor-thin lips radiated mild concern. She seemed to be accusing him of something. But these were silly questions asked by people who didn't know him and probably didn't really know Helen, people they had seen only on brief vacations through the last thirty years. He drank some bourbon. It was easy. Swallow, smile. She waited, as usual, for his usual answer, which he gave with his usual ease.

"Oh, you know Helen. She doesn't much like to travel the way I do. I always want to come and stay a few days and then come back later. That's too hard on Helen. She wants to come and stay a *month*, can you believe that? We couldn't be gone for a month. There'd be no one to take care of the house — Sarah's gone and Bob is always busy." Go ahead and lie, what difference did it make with these people?

Mavis returned his blank stare until she suddenly blinked.

"Well, but you could fly her up and back this year."

Yeah. He had done that before. If Helen had her way she would go every other month. She always had something to say about all the work she had to do and she guessed she really couldn't leave until spring. But then he would let her buy an airplane ticket and she would go.

"Well, to tell you the truth, Mavis, I *am* going to fly Helen up here. She can stay as long as she wants, a month even. As soon as I get this dad-blamed house finished I'll come up too. I'll probably be too tired to drive . . ."

He hadn't thought about this until just now, but it sounded like a good idea. Let Helen come up here for a while, get her away. He had no intention of joining her — that was just something he said to Mavis. He always seemed to say things that surprised him to Mavis. Things that sounded natural in the Sanders house.

Mavis was glad to hear that, indeed she was, and she would be looking forward to it. Now the best thing to do was get some dinner and then everyone had to have some sleep and decide what to do about Billy in the morning. She was Billy's own mother and she was worried to death but there wasn't much anyone could do right then.

So eventually Carlyle was able to sit on the tightly made double bed and take off his shirt, his back corset and his shoes. He winced when he stood up to take off his Bermuda shorts; and he stepped out of them carefully, like a child trying to make no noise. He could hear Mavis's and Pete's low voices from their bedroom down the hall; he wondered whether they did it anymore. There was a time when he could have talked to Pete about that, but that was long ago. When he lay down he realized the mattress was too soft, but he fell asleep almost as soon as he closed his eyes.

He woke to a rapping on the door.

"Carly? You awake?"

He grunted. "Hmm . . . yeah, I'm awake." He felt like a petrified log.

"Listen, I got some news about Billy. Won't have to go to the police, after all. I think I can find him now."

"Oh." He suppressed a groan as he turned over. "That's good."

"Mavis's got coffee ready, and eggs and everything."

"Okay, Pete. Be there in a minute." As he sat up on the edge of the bed he felt such pain that a violent "Ouch!" escaped him. He gritted his teeth, trying to control his breathing.

"You okay, Carly? That old back of yours isn't giving you trouble, is it?"

"Naw, Pete." He forced a chuckle. "I just moved too fast getting up. A little charley horse. It's okay."

"Okay then."

He was glad Pete had remembered that he hated to sleep late. He strapped on the corset as if it could hold the useless parts of him together. When his back felt this way, the corset was like a crab's shell, and he was nothing but tender quivering crab flesh inside it.

Mavis poured coffee for the three of them into pretty flowered cups. The kitchen was bright, the counter tops were clean and shiny. One thing you could say for Mavis—she was a spotless housekeeper. Her trim waist and her clean house made him angry when he thought of Helen. But at least Helen didn't use rouge. If Mavis didn't use rouge and wasn't so nosy, who knows? Pete had met her through her brother Jack who was more Carlyle's friend than Pete's in those days. Could have been Carlyle, just as likely as Pete.

Mavis was pretty then, maybe prettier than Helen, but not as warm. Used to see her strutting by with her parasol on her way home from school, watch her pretend not to notice him while he worked on one of the new houses beginning to fill in along her street, their yards maybe one tenth the size of the grounds owned by Mavis's family. She saw him, all right, and some days, just at the last minute, she would nod, a pert nod, probably just like the nods she gave their maid at home. A lot of the girls were hot after him then because he was handsome — he knew he was handsome, he could tell when he walked into a party and the women looked at him. Even though he was short. They all liked his curly black hair. Back then they thought he was dashing, and he could have gone out with Mavis if he had wanted to. She was there for the asking, before she ever met Pete, but there was something about her that kept Carlyle from asking her.

It was nearly nine o'clock. He couldn't stand to sleep half the morning away. "I didn't mean to sleep so late," he said. "Real comfortable bed." The bed was so soft it had made his back worse.

They were both smiling at him. He could tell they must have had good news about Billy.

Pete was very excited. He had gotten a phone call from a friend who owned a small motel in the area. It seemed the friend had found Billy's name on a wake-up call for eleven that morning. The night clerk had told him that a bunch of kids had had a party there the night before, until all hours.

"Probably kids from that house," Pete said. "Anyway, I'm going over there soon to try and bring him home."

"Makes sense," Carlyle said. He wished that Mavis had served some orange juice. He always liked a glass of cold juice before breakfast.

"Must have been some party. The night clerk just about called the police." Pete was obviously too relieved to worry about that; he thought it was funny. Mavis was quietly drinking her coffee. "Hell, Carly, remember the parties we used to have? Remember the one we had for Ned Sorrell? Boy, was that ever fun!"

"What's old Ned doin' now anyway?" Carlyle asked.

"Well, the old bastard's pushin' seventy, but he's still a regular at the club."

"Oh, seventy's not so old." Didn't Pete know that Carlyle

himself was sixty-five? He didn't expect to be feeling old for some time yet, even though his back had stopped him from playing golf these last few years. He thought suddenly of Duffy, sitting and staring in the boat. Well, Duffy *had* been old; he had begun to seem *old*, although so gradually that it had not been noticeable while it was happening. But Duffy had a slight build. Ned Sorrell was big, and husky, like Carlyle himself.

Pete was getting up to go. "Listen, you two," Carlyle said, "I'll be out running errands today, but I thought I'd drop back about six, see if you folks feel like being taken out to dinner. Billy too, if he wants to come."

Mavis and Pete exchanged glances. But Carlyle always took them out to dinner when he visited. "Hey, listen," he said easily, "we can always make it some other time . . ."

"Oh, no, Carly, that would be great," Pete said. "That would be just great. Except we thought maybe we'd take *you* out tonight — and Billy, all four of us. Thought we'd celebrate at the club. We already made reservations."

Carlyle thought it was kind of odd; especially now, when Pete certainly didn't need to be a good host.

"Well, here you are feeding me and putting me up and now you want to take me out to dinner too! Well, I'm no fool. You got a deal. Of course I'm not forgetting you want that property. Maybe you're just trying to butter me up!"

He laughed then, a clear, genuine laugh, so contagious that Pete and even Mavis joined in. It was ridiculous even to suggest that Pete would butter him up. If Pete offered five thousand an acre, it was because he honestly believed that that was what the land was worth. And Pete didn't need to worry about what price he paid for the land he bought. They were really nicer than he had thought, the Sanders. He felt a sudden prick of guilt for his thoughts about Mavis and her rouge.

Carlyle sat at the table drinking coffee while Mavis went down the long carpeted hallway to see Pete off at the front door. He did not hear the door close and gave a slight start as she appeared suddenly in front of him again, holding out the morning newspaper.

"Maybe you want to look at this, Carlyle. Looks like a hurricane is going to hit Florida."

There were always hurricanes. Most of them never came close. But that was the way they sold newspapers. He glanced skeptically at the headline. "I doubt it's anything to worry about," he said.

She sat down opposite him. "I hope not," she said vaguely. She was looking out the kitchen window, past the long back yard to the row of trees at the bottom of the hill. She was worrying about Billy. In the sports section there was a story about the local high school team at Billy's high school that had replaced the one he and Pete had gone to so many years ago. The story was about the great hopes for the upcoming season. Carlyle found it boring. Of course when he and Pete went to school there was no football team. He put the paper down and pushed his chair back, gathering himself carefully into position to get up.

"I just know he's caught cold. Out there in the damp half the night. He could catch pneumonia." She was really speaking to herself.

"Oh, at that age a kid doesn't catch cold, Mavis. A night or two outside doesn't hurt him. Maybe you don't remember. I ran away too, when I was his age." He paused until she looked up at him. "Yeah, I ran away twice. The second time I didn't come back, I was on my own. But the first time I might have been younger than Billy, and I stayed outside in a lot worse weather than this, and I didn't catch nothin' but a whippin' from the old man!" He smiled, but Mavis frowned. He wondered if he had said something wrong.

"From *your* father that figures," she said.

"The old man was tough," he began, before he realized how much her remark shocked him. "Yes, tough," he went on, "but he wasn't so bad. He wasn't so bad. Anyway I didn't get sick." His only desire was to get away from her. He mumbled his thanks for the breakfast and left.

They always looked down on the old man, these North Carolina people, because he didn't live in a big house on a big piece of land and because he was a failure in business—one business right after the other, four failures before he was through. Maybe it was poor timing. Maybe just fate. But the old man worked hard, he did his best. He wasn't lazy like a lot of these high-class spoiled white trash. You had to give him credit for that, even if you hated him. And Carlyle had hated him — because his mother had worked herself to death trying to help out, because he had a bad farm on bad land and no talent for business, but most of all he hated him because the old man was mean and nasty. He used his whip on his son for any little thing, any excuse. He hated him until the old man grew thin and stooped — then he could pity him. By that time Carlyle had made more money on his first business than his father had lost on all four failures together.

He had forgotten how angry he got when these North Carolina people looked down their noses at the old man while they admired his son, the son who flashed enough green to make them respect him. As he backed his car out of the driveway, he considered turning down their dinner invitation and moving to a motel. But nothing would be gained by that. He did not want to take the trouble to tell any of them how he felt, it was easier to let it go. It was easier to behave normally and pretend they were all old friends.

He drove down Waterford and took old Woods Hill Road out to the country. It was the shortest route to Green's Road and it also went right past Helen's sister's house, and all the fast food restaurants and 7-11s that had changed this part of the county forever. As he drove he realized suddenly that he had passed his sister-in-law's place without noticing it. Every time he came here for a few days he realized all over again how wise he had been to move to Florida. If he had stayed here he could not have avoided the sisters-in-law, the brothers-in-law, and even Helen's crazy mother — the stubborn old woman who ran her farm singlehandedly for thirty years and who was the only woman who Carlyle had ever truly hated. He hated her while he respected her sheer courage.

She had been his natural enemy while she lived, and no one would have been surprised if she had outlived him. But she had finally died, three years ago, at eighty-seven, and even he had been surprised at how her death had upset him. He had never set foot in that woman's house after he had taken Helen from it and he did not go with Helen to the funeral. He had put her on a plane and let her stay an extra month to help cope with the legal complications. The old lady had been able to leave some money to her children, even though when her sickly husband had died thirty years before he had left her almost nothing but his old family name. Carlyle had long suspected there had been some kind of run-in long ago between his father and Helen's mother but he never did find out anything about it, and after the old woman died he felt like he had lost something. Sure, he had succeeded in taking Helen away from her, but in some ways the old woman won out in the end. Even though he'd taken her down to Florida, his wife stayed in close communication with her family and he had had to send Helen back up to Carolina every year.

There was little traffic on these roads, even now — one advantage over Florida, anyway. Helen had hated moving there, she had begged him not to do it, but after he made it clear that *he* was moving whether she came along or not, she packed up the children and joined him. But she never forgave him. She didn't have to put it into words: he knew it, he was reminded of it every time she came back from a visit to Carolina. Helen was still her mother's daughter; the old woman knew he couldn't change that, wherever he took her. He gathered up the mucus that had been accumulating in his throat and spat out the window.

Helen loved these rolling green hills, narrow winding roads. Wasn't anything like the Florida coast. He had probably loved this place too when he was a kid on the farm, but not after he grew up and knew the place more for its people than for its hills. He turned onto Green's Road and was relieved to see it was still semi-rural — there were only a few houses here, spread far apart.

It had been years since he had driven down this road, since he had bothered to notice what the old place looked like. The farm had changed hands many times since his father had had it. The chicken coops and the small barn, destroyed long ago, had never been rebuilt. He slowed the car as he approached. The long dirt driveway that used to take him *forever* to walk down was paved now with cement. And the modern brick house with its tidy shutters was not at all like the old wooden house where he had grown up. He was pleased to see that whoever was living there now was keeping the yard up. After all that rain, his lawn in Florida would be wild with growth and hard to cut when he got back.

It looked like the present owners were using the farm land only for their pleasure horses, as people did nowadays. A nice big place, and no worries about farming it. Of course it wasn't as big as when his daddy first bought it. He had gradually sold off land as the farm yielded less and less and he tried to finance one business after another.

Carlyle stopped the car and stared at the places where he guessed the chicken coop and the barn had been. It was strange; he could not remember with certainty. He tried to imagine them, the structure of the coop, the outline of the barn; they were clear in his mind, but they would not come clear on the land. He could not fit the two together. Maybe they belonged now only to his private vision, because it had been so long since they were destroyed, since his father had let the land go.

"Well, old man," he murmured, "if you were still alive, I'd tell you I've never had to sell land, I've never been in the kind of bind you were in. I sell when I want to sell, I don't *have* to, no thanks to you."

Traffic was approaching. He started the car, pulled down the visor and drove on.

In the old days, to get to the cabin you took a rough two-lane road that narrowed into one lane and was unpaved for the last five miles. He had wanted a place where he could be far away from people, where it would always be quiet, and he had chosen the most thickly wooded part of the county. He knew it would still be thickly wooded, and quiet, but the route had changed. They had built a big interstate which you had to take to the Shallow Ditch exit. Shallow Ditch was a four-lane paved highway, and it led directly to what was left of the old road. Once you got off Shallow Ditch and took the old road, you were within a mile of the lot. He thought, briefly, of driving past the other house, the small house he and Helen had lived in the first five years they were married. But he had been back to see it before, and that was enough. He had sold it when they moved to Florida; the children had been so young then that they hardly remembered it. But the cabin was different, that was before everything, and he wanted to see that property once more before he let it go to Pete Sanders.

He left Green's Road and went back toward town, following the signs to I-26. There was a hitchhiker at the entrance to the highway; involuntarily he veered slightly to the left and sped up. He wondered whether Billy was back at home by now with Pete and Mavis.

After he had gone a mile or so he realized that the hitchhiker had reminded him of Billy. He hadn't seen the kid for three or four years. But of course it couldn't be Billy—Billy was in a motel over on highway 25; Pete had gone to pick him up. So it couldn't be Billy. Not that it would matter all that much if it was. Be better for all concerned if they just let him go. He'd be back soon enough. On the other hand, what if it *was* Billy? He looked for exit signs. Billy had light hair. He might be taller now than Carlyle remembered him.

He would just let it go. It wasn't his responsibility. He turned on the radio, but all he could get was rock music and a gospel station full of static. He kept on driving, but the thing was beginning to nag at him. What if it was Billy, and the kid didn't come back? Then there would be something to hide. That's what it would be: hiding. Well, wasn't this just dandy! If he pretended he hadn't seen what he knew he *had* seen—whether or not it turned out to be Billy—he wouldn't be fooling himself.

Once he had made up his mind, it seemed to take forever to find an exit. He pulled into the first gas station he saw and dialed Mavis. One quick way to find out whether Pete had found Billy. If he had, he would have to make up some stupid story to explain the call. A game, but one he could live with.

Pete answered with a gruff hello.

"Yeah, listen, how is everything? Just thought I'd check."

"Oh, Carlyle. It's you." Pete sounded relieved. "Things aren't so good, I guess. There wasn't anybody in that motel room—just bottles and glasses and trash. They must have been giving him a farewell party. He's long gone by now, I guess. We told the police." He paused. "I thought that might be them when you called."

Carlyle glanced around automatically to make sure no one was in earshot. He felt like a kid about to tattle.

"Uh, listen Pete. I'm out here off I-26, maybe ten miles north of town. Um, I saw this kid hitching. And it looked like it might a been Billy."

Pete couldn't seem to decide which questions to ask.

"*Where? When?* You mean you *saw* him? I don't understand why you didn't stop and pick him up. You mean you just left him there? When *was* this —"

He had not expected anger. He could feel himself flushing.

"Now listen, Pete, calm down. I wasn't sure it was Billy." *And even if it was, I don't have any responsibility to pick up your runaway for you.* He fought to control himself. "It was just a couple minutes ago. I was coming onto I-26 from Perkins Boulevard. Right on the entrance ramp. Might be him, might not. Anyway, I thought you picked him up at that motel."

"Yeah, I thought I would." Pete calmed down a bit. He no longer breathed heavily into the phone. "I don't know. You really weren't sure it was him?"

There was still anger in his voice. Accusation. As if *they* hadn't screwed it up in the first place. As if *they* weren't lucky he had even bothered to call when he knew the best thing was to let the kid go.

"No, it didn't hit me until I was long past him. It was just a couple minutes ago."

"Did you notice what he was wearing?"

"Not really. Jeans I guess. A jacket or something and one of those camping things, you know — look, I'll go back and see if it's him —"

"No, it's okay. I'm on my way. Maybe I can get there before somebody picks him up. Or the police spot him."

A pause. Pete kept breathing into the phone. It was a relief that Pete had not asked him to go back and pick up the kid. Maybe he figured that would be a bad idea from anybody's point of view.

"Listen Carly . . ."

"Yeah?"

"Uh, thanks. You know. Really. Thanks."

He pulled off the highway and found the old road to the cabin. He was struck by the quiet. After the steady roar of traffic on the highway, after Pete's loud voice on the phone, after the noise of his tires on the rutted dirt road, he parked the car in the narrow lane and sat, feeling the quiet as if it breathed all around him. Time had slowed down here. It seemed as if you had to be careful not to make any move that would break the stillness.

He did not know why he had come. Why should he have bothered? He knew perfectly well what this place looked like, what condition it was likely to be in, what it was worth. On either side of the dirt lane that wound up the hill to the clearing, the lot was covered with trees and thick undergrowth. He was surprised that the clearing was not littered with junk and that the vine-covered cabin had not been damaged by vandals. The lane itself was overgrown and barely passable, nearly hidden by years of disuse; maybe that was why. The stillness began to make him uneasy. He felt threatened. He was not afraid of any man and he had never felt uneasy on his own land. He reached for the ignition key. It was foolish to have come. But he hesitated. Foolish to come all this way and not have a look around. Slowly he got out of the car, leaving the keys in the ignition.

Kudzu, potato vine. It covered the old cabin all the way from the sagging roof to the pine trees on either side. The trees were like two anchors suspending the cabin in a green hammock which had sunk to the ground under its weight. That was how they had built the Golden Gate Bridge to San Francisco, although he had never seen it. All that weight, suspended. He wouldn't trust it, if he lived there. The vine had even gone after the dogwood tree in front of the cabin—a tree he had thought would never make it when he first saw it more than twenty years ago. Now it looked strong and healthy. It would be a shame if Pete Sanders decided to remove it. Carlyle walked to the tree, grabbed at the vine wrapped around its trunk and pulled hard. After a moment he let go. No use fighting potato vine.

In the spaces between the vine's large irregular leaves he could see two or three panes in each of the two windows at the front of the cabin that remained unbroken. In the places where the cabin wall was visible, he could see green and gray lichen in the dark wood. Between the two windows, the door, mottled like the rest with lichen, stood ajar. There was a pile of rocks in front of the door. He kicked some of them aside; ants and insects scattered from underneath.

With his foot he brushed aside the leaves that had accumulated on the threshold. The door was heavy on rusty hinges. He leaned into it, pressing his shoulder against the rough, weathered wood. The door moved barely an inch, scraping the floor boards, and then stopped. He could not move it further. He reminded himself to be careful not to strain his back. He stepped back and paused, surprised at how heavily he was breathing. Then, carefully, he secured his stance and threw his right leg against the door. His back pulled, but he ignored it. He pushed his shoulder against the door, using his entire body as leverage. This time the door moved a few more inches, making an opening wide enough for him to squeeze through sideways.

He stood, waiting for his eyes to grow accustomed to the darkness. There was a strong odor of mildew and dust. How long, he wondered, was it since anyone had come in here. He had not set foot inside that door for ten years . . . more than ten years. Long ago he had stopped bringing Helen and the kids here. For the first few vacations, yes. But then the cabin was too small and inconvenient for them; they wanted to be close to Helen's family. The last few trips he had dropped them at his sister-in-law's and gone on to stay alone, either at the cabin or at a motel. When his friends found out he was in town, invariably one of them would come up to him at the club and insist he stay with them. And he would, for a night or two, before heading back. He never stayed long, and they all said they didn't get to see enough of him. Pete and George Granger, the best golfer at the club after Carlyle stopped playing, and Mack Patterson, the one man Carlyle would never attempt to arm-wrestle. Mack's arms were so thick his wife had to alter every one of his shirts.

And there were others. He had probably stayed in ten different homes here over the years. Got drunk and made them laugh, and they said they loved him. What they really loved were the good meals he bought them, and all those drinks. Not that they couldn't afford to buy these themselves, but they all seemed to think he was richer than they were. He had never been able to figure that out. They were different from his Florida friends. Some of these people went way back with him and yet they made him angry sometimes in a way that Duffy never did. He felt impatient and apart from them. They acted as if they knew him better than they really did. Assuming things. Smiling in a kind of superior way and underneath, the threat, the threat. *I know, Carlyle. You can't fool me.* But they didn't know and they didn't care. Duffy had never done that. Even Nelson never made him feel that way. Whatever he did was okay by them. Maybe he really was one man to Pete and Mavis and another to Duffy. He had known Pete, George and Mack for more than forty years, but that didn't make him feel any closer to them. It was too many years since they had really known each other, or wanted to. Now what he hated in them was the pretense, the falsity of their smiles and their hospitality.

When his eyes adjusted he noticed how little the cabin had changed—or rather how everything had changed but how little difference it seemed to make. The roof had fallen in and just in front of him a long beam lay diagonally across the room. Bits of sunlight came through the broken roof, speckling the floors and walls. The floor was littered with broken branches of various sizes. The bed was still there, pushed into a corner, covered with branches, pine cones and other debris. The bed and two wooden chairs with broken seats were all the furniture that remained. He was surprised to see that the pump handle was still there, on the wall that had served as a kitchen. He ducked under the fallen beam and went to the sink. Something fluttered above him; he turned to see a bird fly gracefully through the opening in the roof. The cabin could offer no protection against the outside now, but it had been tight as a drum when he had brought Helen here for the honeymoon. He wondered what she would say if she saw it like this. If she would want to know.

He tried the pump, but the handle would not budge. Frozen tight with rust and disuse, or perhaps the well had gone dry. But no, Pete would have made certain that the well was still good before he offered for the land. Here at the makeshift sink—nothing more, really, than a tin bucket with a drain to the outside—Helen and he had washed themselves and brushed their teeth and done the dishes. And Helen had washed her hair. She had left the bed and pumped the ice-cold water up while she leaned forward and let her dark curls fall into the sink. She didn't scream or make any noise when the ice-cold water struck her scalp. Some woman, he had thought, watching her pale, slender neck curving under the pump. She had been some woman then.

She had been only too happy to come here then, to leave Washington and go back to Townsend with him. If her brother's friend hadn't gotten that job for her, working for the junior representative from Carolina, they might never have gotten married. He had dated her a couple of times and the old lady hadn't seemed real happy about it; she might have tried to forbid Helen to see him at all except that she knew Helen was leaving soon for Washington, so she thought the whole thing would just fizzle out. But by then Carlyle knew that Helen Jones was different from other women he had fallen for. He waited a while and then went back to dating Eugenia. But every time he gave her a present—no matter how expensive it was, or how much of a surprise it was intended to be—she would take it from him and say "Oh, *thank* you," like a telephone operator or a bank teller. She acted as if it was something she had misplaced that he had found for her, and she always put it away in her bedroom. She did not have Helen's warmth. Finally he realized that Helen was not going to stay in Washington forever, and that his only chance to see her without the old lady breathing down their necks was to go on up to Washington. He told no one where he was going, just left the house he was working on and went after her.

It had cost him plenty to stay in Washington that first visit, but later on he made some investments that turned out to be worthwhile. Motels. That was where the money was then. He discovered that he didn't like the motel business when he tried to run one himself, but at least it kept him busy, and that way it did not look as though he were driving back and forth from Townsend to Washington just for Helen, and it wasn't just for Helen. He wondered how much it wasn't for Helen: how much something besides Helen herself made him seek her out and drove him to marry her.

The pump handle felt cold in the quiet warm cabin. He put his forehead against the handle and rubbed it lightly back and forth.

A cockroach crawled out of the drain and suddenly stopped. Probably roaches everywhere in the place. He straightened up. Cobwebs in all the corners, some with curled-up bodies of spiders. The two front windows were bare, but the back window, near the bed, still had shreds of curtains, once pale blue, now aged a dirty grey. Helen Jones, whose mother had managed to send her to a good private women's college, had hemmed those curtains on her honeymoon. When she was in Washington, she had enjoyed being near a big city, going to museums and the library, saving the money she earned for a good pair of shoes or a nice suit made in New York or Paris. But she was homesick. Every time he went to see her, she asked him about Carolina. Later, when he told her about the cabin she asked him for the window measurements; she was surprised that he knew them by heart. Well, he had built the place, hadn't he? He ought to know every inch of it. She had looked at him with the look she gave him back then, a kind of shy admiration. She bought the fabric at the Hecht Company. The curtains were not quite finished when it was time for her to pack, so she finished sewing the hems the afternoon after her wedding night. When the curtains were hung, he could no longer see the rain, but he could hear it.

An old broom was standing in the corner. He thought of sweeping out the cabin with it, but the broom was covered with dust and cobwebs, and even if he cleared out all the debris, more would sift in within a day or two. Even with the roof damage, which was to be expected, the place held up pretty well over the years. But he did not feel proud of it. Even the old memory of its better days did not bring him satisfaction. Just a crummy old cabin. He ducked under the beam again and squeezed out the door.

The sunlight was painful at first. He shielded his eyes and breathed deeply, taking in the fresh air as if he had just come up from under water. These three acres were worth a good seven thousand apiece. It was one of the prettiest locations you'd ever find. Standing in front of the cabin, he could see the entire valley below him. There were mountains behind, but this was high enough, easily reached and private, with clean, cool crisp mountain air. No smell of salt which you took for granted in Florida. For a moment, as he looked at the tree-covered hillsides and down at the valley, the dark blues and greens of Carolina, he thought it might make a difference if he were a younger man. But now he saw it as a stranger would, an intruder on his own land. He would probably never come up here again. He could see pretty views on postcards. There was nothing for him here.

Pete's Cadillac Sedan de Ville ate gasoline, but it gave the smoothest ride Carlyle had ever had in any car. It was pleasant to be able to sit back and watch the houses and trees fly past the window. Pete and Mavis talked about the weather and recent events at the club. They were relaxed now that Billy was home; Pete had found him right where Carlyle had seen him, and the boy had agreed to go home without much fuss.

It wasn't necessary to join the conversation; they seemed to sense that Carlyle wasn't in a talkative mood. He closed his eyes and dozed off and woke suddenly, startled and embarrassed. Mavis and Pete were still chatting, occasionally glancing at the back seat.

"So long as he stays and finishes school," Pete was saying. "After that, we'll see. He might change his mind about college, who knows?"

College or no college, it didn't much matter. Carlyle could tell them about that if he wanted to bother. Everybody was so dead set on sending the kids to college. He couldn't see where it did much good. It hadn't helped Helen much that he could see. Or Bob. And Sarah could have been a secretary without going to that big university. Sarah had carried on so when he sold that beach property to the development company. He doubted even Sarah would care if she knew he was selling the Carolina land to Pete Sanders.

"Carlyle," Mavis said, "you know on the news tonight they said that hurricane *is* going to hit Florida. The whole west coast is on alert."

She did not add, *I think you should call Helen,* but he understood her. He responded only to her words.

"Probably fizzle out at the last minute, or turn the other way. You never know about those things." He doubted it would hit land, but nonetheless he felt a bit relieved that not enough work had been done yet on the Beaumont house for much damage to occur. So far he had managed to have only the block masons, the rough-in plumber, the flooring specialist. Scovill and another carpenter he had recommended had come in to do the lintels, but they had not been able to put on the roof yet because the rain had started as soon as the lintels and rebars were set. Carlyle was not sure whether they had done a better job than the masons could have done with the lintels, but he had been keeping a sharp eye on Scovill and Scovill knew it.

Mavis did not pursue the subject, and he sat back and watched the final curve of the road before the clubhouse came into view. *His* clubhouse: he had built it more than thirty years ago. It was the building which, more than any other, had made his reputation in the area, the reputation which had followed him all the way to Florida, the name he had had to equal every single time he built anything afterwards. That was the name this clubhouse had given him: Simpson, the best you can get. Look at that job he did on the country club. Right down to the wainscoting, that building's solid as a bomb shelter, classic clean lines and trim perfect as a picture. He watched for the red clubhouse with the white columns. The board of directors had suggested pillars, but he had said no, he did not want the building to look like a Southern plantation. Now he saw it, high on its hill overlooking the golf course and he allowed himself a flash of the old pride.

The parking lot was nearly full.

"Bring back memories?" Pete asked.

He knew, as he always had, that he would never build another building half as good.

They bypassed the large restaurant and walked toward the private dining room. Something was going on. When Pete held the double doors open for him, Carlyle hesitated to enter the room. But he followed Mavis, knowing now what was coming.

People were standing, and applauding; stopping in mid-sentence, probably to rise and turn toward him. He felt himself flushing and was suddenly conscious of Pete and Mavis pausing on either side of him, waiting for him to take his seat at the center of the long table at the opposite end of the big room.

"I'll be damned, you sneaky bastard. You really took me in."

If Pete answered, Carlyle did not hear him. He was looking at the men he had played golf with, some he had had arguments with about the building and, later, about the way they ran the club. Some he couldn't remember. Helen's brother Lawrence, the tall, skinny lawyer was standing unsmiling at the end of the long right-hand table. He was a few years younger than Carlyle — and a pretty fair golfer. He was always a good man to have on a foursome because he didn't talk much, he didn't play a bad game, and he was smart. Carlyle used to watch him when the other guys were shooting the bull. But when it came to something serious, Lawrence would speak up and everyone would listen. But Lawrence had stopped being friendly when Carlyle had moved to Florida.

They walked down to the head table, and Carlyle sat between Mavis and Pete. Pete stood up and the room grew quiet.

"I guess everybody knows why we're here. This rotten old miser —uh — I mean of course our past president and co-founder and seven times low gross winner, the man who built this building — is back with us tonight. He doesn't visit us very often any more, so we thought we would take this opportunity to renew old ties. Especially since — as we all know — it's the thirty-fifth anniversary of the founding of this club."

Carlyle sipped some ice water, his face burning with unaccustomed embarrassment. Did they know he had not remembered the date? There seemed to be nowhere he could look without feeling uncomfortable. They were all focused on him, noticing, maybe, that his grey hair had turned white in places, that he had put on weight. How much could they see when he was sitting like this, most of him behind the table and his red sport coat hiding the flab? There were women in this room, long since old and gone to pot, who would be looking at him and still thinking he was handsome, no matter what age did to his body.

Pete stopped talking. There was polite applause. Champagne was poured, and they drank a toast. To him. Carlyle felt hot. They expected him to say something, so he stood up and thanked them: it was a pleasant surprise, nice to see all of them again, and maybe again, in another thirty-five years. He really had nothing to say, and he sank back and drank some champagne.

Waiters brought prime roast beef and lobster. Pete had spared no expense. Carlyle still felt warm; he wanted to get up and take off his sport coat, but more than that he wanted to avoid calling more attention to himself. He stayed put.

They gave him some time, at least, to eat before they started coming up to him, clapping him on the shoulder, talking at him so fast he could hardly make sense of what they said, trying to catch up on this and that, and who won the last tournament in Florida, and always, always, they asked about Helen. Why wasn't she with him? How was she doing? Her health, her eyes, why they never got to see her. An obligatory mention of the kids, but always Helen. He had come up here alone because he wanted to come up here alone, and if he had wanted to have Helen with him, he would have brought her. But he mumbled and laughed and teased and some- how blundered his way through — there were some people whose names he could remember.

But they all knew him. Not just because of the clubhouse, either. They remembered details he had long since forgotten; they could probably tell a stranger more about his time in Carolina than he could himself.

Lawrence Jones did not come over to say hello. When everyone had finished eating, they sat politely, waiting for him to say a few more words.

"That was good roast beef, Pete. The whole dinner was good. You really did it up fine, just like the going away party you all threw for me way back. But you're not getting me to stand up and make an ass of myself again."

Pete, Mavis, and the others who heard it smiled.

"Guess Carlyle's still too sober to talk," Pete announced. "I hope they've got plenty of Wild Turkey back there."

Those who didn't want to stay or didn't like to drink came up to him to say goodbye before he'd started on his second glass. Two couples he didn't know or had forgotten, and a few more he did remember but didn't like much. Then Ned Sorrell.

"I hear you still play some, Ned." He stood with his arm resting on the bar. Ned, who was six feet tall, seemed to be growing stooped.

"Yeah, I still do. But I sure don't shoot the same scores I used to. Couple weeks ago I shot an eighty, but that's my only decent score in a long time. What about you, Carlyle?"

"Nah. It's the damn back trouble, you know."

Ned nodded. There were big, loose wrinkles in his skin, and his cheeks trembled when he nodded. His red hair had turned a dirty white, like the hair of some women who were once dishwater blondes. His skin had that yellowed look to it, with brown spots. His skin would never turn pasty white, even if did not spend much time in the sun. Carlyle's own wrinkles were tighter and sharper. Ned was more like Helen, the skin a bit loose about the bones.

"Hey, Carly," Ned said, laughing, "remember the time we took that cow to the school and turned it loose? Scared everybody half to death! You damn near had to carry that cow on home. It's a wonder your back didn't give out on you years ago. All that construction work and horsing around and golfing and chasing women did it."

Carlyle laughed. He remembered the pranks. They were the good things. But Ned and Pete and all the rest of them were not the same anymore, and they seemed to realize it. Maybe that's why when he came back to visit all they wanted to do was talk about the fooling around.

"Yeah. Guess you're right. But I think the golfing is what did it."

Ned stopped laughing and looked straight at him.

"You were the best, Carly. The best president we ever had here, too."

Pete had come up, and heard him. "Now, Ned, don't start on that. You know how this bourbon guzzler hates that kind of talk. And *you* were the one who put the snake in the men's john, right here at the club."

"Yeah, it sure was you, Ned Sorrell," Carlyle said. "I never saw Mack come out of there so fast." He unbuttoned his sports coat. "He thought *I* did it."

"Still does, probably," Pete said. "No one ever bothered to set him straight on it. Shit, Carlyle, it fits in with all the other tricks you pulled."

"Like the year he hid all the trophies," Ned said.

"Or the time he let the air out of your tires when you were on that date with Sally Loggins."

"Okay, okay, don't remind him and get him riled at me again," Carlyle told Pete. He grinned. Even Ned, as mad as he got, had thought it was funny. Carlyle took off his coat and hung it on a chair.

"Shit, Carly. If you'd stayed up here the way you should have, no telling what else you'd have pulled. Ask me, Townsend's damn lucky you left," Ned said. He was kidding. "And we got no more monstrosities like this bullshit club you built here, either."

There was an awkward silence. Pete told the bartender to refill their glasses.

"Yeah. Only favor I ever did ya, Ned. That was leavin'," Carlyle said.

Later, they wrestled. He drank enough whiskey to dull the pain in his back slightly at least, then he went with Ned to the long dinner table, and pushed back the white linen tablecloth, bunching it up to make room.

Ned was still a fair golfer, but he wasn't much of a wrestler. The air had grown thick with smoke and people were beginning to leave. They came to wish him well and say goodbye, clapping him on the back, or smiling timidly. "We sure miss you, Carly. No matter how long it's been, nobody forgets things around the club were a lot livelier when you were here."

He smiled back at them, promised to come back up to see them again soon. Then he pushed Ned's arm to the table with little effort. Ned sat back and rubbed his shoulder, looking him straight in the eye.

"Okay. Enough of the nice guy, mister."

They wrestled again and Carlyle beat him again, but not before a pain shot up his back and Pete saw him wince.

"That was tough," he lied to Ned.

"Didn't mean to hurt you, Carly. How come your arms are still so damned strong when you don't play golf any more?"

"I don't know. Guess because I wrestle right much. And I do all that lawn work. Carrying stuff all the time, I guess."

"Hell, Ned, you don't know nothin'. It's from dancing with all those young chicks down in Florida."

"Yeah," Ned said, "and then you do your pushups over those young chicks, right?"

Carlyle could feel the heat in his face; he knew he was blushing.

They all laughed, glancing at the bar. Lawrence Jones was still there, and they wouldn't want Lawrence to hear this kind of talk. But Lawrence was involved in a discussion with Mavis. Mavis was probably telling him all about Billy.

"Yeah, Carly, I'm gonna come on down there next winter. You better be prepared. I want to lie on that pretty white sand and look at all those blondies wearing suntan oil."

"Sure, Ned. All the blondies past eighty, you mean. Guess that would be all right."

The three of them could laugh now because Ned's wife had been dead for ten years and Ned loved to pretend that he was a swinging widower. He didn't fool anyone and Carlyle supposed it did no harm to play the little game.

"Hey, I get to wrestle the winner," Pete said. He took Ned's place. Ned went off to see some other people. Carlyle took Pete's palm in his, gripping it hard, hoping Pete wasn't any better than Ned, but also hoping that Pete would not fake it and let him win because he'd seen him wince.

They'd been at it a few minutes when he heard behind him the unmistakable bass voice of Lawrence Jones.

"Arm wrestling, huh?" Lawrence walked around to where Carlyle could see him, and stood behind Pete.

Lawrence said it as if he didn't think much of arm wrestling.

"Well, Lawrence. It's been a long time."

"Yes, it has, Carlyle. They tell me the party's a surprise, because you forgot about the anniversary. What are you doing up here this time? Come up to play in a tournament, or what?"

"No tournaments, Lawrence." He kept Pete's arm steady, but couldn't push it over. He could feel the strength in Pete's hand, but he was not sure if it was all Pete had or if he was waiting. "I haven't played golf in a while now. Just came up to see about some business."

Lawrence squinted, probably because of the smoke. He was tall and had a longish face, with many fine wrinkles around his eyes and across his forehead. He looked like he did a lot of looking and thinking. Lawrence was still in his fifties and his dark hair was still full and wavy, the way Helen's had been before she started getting beauty parlor curls and old woman's frizz.

Carlyle looked at Pete: he was concentrating, or pretending to concentrate on the wrestling. Just at this moment he did not want to tell Lawrence Jones that he was selling that hill property. He began to feel uneasy. He wished Lawrence would go away, or at least sit down if he stayed, and stop squinting down at him.

"How's Helen?"

That was what Lawrence had come to ask; it was the only question Lawrence ever really asked. All this time and no change.

"Oh, she's fine. Her arthritis gives her some trouble now and then, and I guess you know about the cataracts." He didn't wait for Lawrence to ask whether she could drive. "She still drives to the grocery store and to church. She's overcautious, but she drives."

Lawrence's high forehead wrinkled up and he opened his mouth to say something, but he seemed to think better of it, and took a large gulp of his drink instead. Probably gin and tonic. Lawrence and his one gin and tonic: never more than one.

"And how's Alice, Lawrence?" Alice had been a real invalid for years; she never went with him anywhere in the evenings. Maybe that was why Lawrence stayed home most of the time.

The tall, nervous man spoke in a dead monotone.

"The same."

Carlyle began to wonder if Lawrence was a little drunk. He himself had had a few drinks, but the bourbon had not affected him yet; he could still feel the dull ache in his lower back. Pete's arm was still resisting his own with solid strength and no sign of weariness.

"Well, you seem to be in pretty good shape yourself, Carlyle."

He wasn't sure he liked Lawrence's tone of voice, but he avoided his eyes and looked at Pete as he answered.

"Yeah, I get around all right. Do just about everything but play golf."

Suddenly Pete spoke. "Guess we might even talk you into playing a few holes one of these days, anyhow, huh, Carly?"

Carlyle grinned a little. The room was much too warm.

"Yeah, I guess you might. Not this trip, though."

Pete pushed his arm to the table, slowly but firmly.

"Another drink, Carlyle?" He was off to the bar before Carlyle could answer.

"Well, the *nerve* of that good-for-nothing stockholder!" He rubbed his arm in mock pain. "Guess this ain't no place for me anymore: I can't even beat Pete Sander!"

He laughed, but Lawrence just stood there and downed his drink. Carlyle got up carefully from the table.

"Too warm in here, anyway," he mumbled. "Going out for some fresh air."

He turned and went for the door. Pete caught him on his way out and said, "You're not mad at me, are you?"

"Of course not, you young punk. I'm just goin' out for some air. Let me know when you and Mavis are ready to leave, all right?"

"Sure. I guess in just a few minutes. Mavis is tired — you know, all that strain the last few days."

He nodded and went out of the dining room, down the wide hall with freshly polished wood floors, checking the wainscoting to make sure everything was clean. The paint was new enough, and the hall looked good. On the wall there was a plaque marking the year the building was constructed and the fact that he had built it, he, Carlyle Simpson, founder and president and winner of the tournament seven consecutive years. But that was so long ago. He wanted people to remember that he had built the place, but the plaque made him nervous. It was too much like a spotlight, say, on just one part of you, or a photograph taken when you were still young, so young you weren't aware that the photograph would someday make you proud and embarrass you. He would hate to have to look at the plaque every day or even every week, as much as he had wanted it there in the first place. He had not imagined, when he was still green with his first pride, that recognition would ever give him any feeling but pleasure.

He went outside and stood on the rear porch, his hands hanging over the white railing, which, unlike the well-preserved interior of the building, needed paint. The clubhouse had been built into the hill, with the dining room on the second floor, so that now he looked over the railing at the back porch and down on the patio below. They had replaced the patio furniture several times; this furniture was different from the furniture he had seen on his last visit. He decided he liked it: it was wrought iron, painted white; the fringed

umbrellas over the tables were floral prints in subdued tones of blue
and pink and yellow. Yellow always looked good with white.

The french doors behind him opened; he did not need to turn to
see who it was. Pete would have started talking right away. Lawrence Jones, the successful lawyer, was the one who waited to
speak. Nothing to do but wait and see what the man wanted. Carlyle
exhaled deeply and felt for a cigar in his shirt pocket; he'd had to
remember to pick up his coat before he left the club.

"Nice out here," Lawrence said.

Carlyle lit the cigar, taking his time establishing the burn.

"So have you been having a good old time with the boys, Carlyle?" It was a statement rather than a question. "Yeah. A good old
time up here while the hurricane hits down in Florida. Just like you,
I guess."

Carlyle did not answer right away; he looked out into the darkness hiding the golf course.

"What are you talking about, Lawrence? Maybe you'd better go
back inside."

"Sure, sure. Go back inside and never say a word to Carlyle
Simpson about the bastard he's been to my sister all these years.
Well, maybe I've had enough to drink tonight and maybe I *will* say
something. I've had almost as much to drink as you for once and
maybe I'll be sorry, but I don't care."

Carlyle said nothing, but he gripped the moist railing, feeling
his body tense.

"Yeah, the last few times you were up here you left Helen and
the kids with Mary as usual and let's see, that one time, it was five
dollars you gave Helen. Five dollars and you didn't show up there
for nearly a week, when you were ready to go back to Florida. You
were throwing money around here every day at some bar like you
are every day down in Florida, I guess, buying everyone drinks, and
forgetting your own wife and kids for a week. Or should I say a
lifetime." Lawrence moved to the railing. "You promised to take
them to the country, you promised to take them all kinds of places,
but you never showed up and you didn't leave them any money so
they could do anything themselves."

Lawrence Jones was bitter; it was the bitterness of old age, and

Lawrence was too young for that. Lawrence must have changed a lot since the old woman had died, and maybe now he was taking it upon himself to speak for her. But Carlyle did not have to put up with it.

"I guess Mary took 'em wherever they needed to go."

"I guess *so*." Lawrence drew out the "so;" it was maddening. He was standing just a foot away from Carlyle now, and he leaned forward and placed both of his hands on the railing. "So then you'd show up all of a sudden and expect them to be ready to leave in ten minutes. Always at least two days earlier than you'd told them. Every time you came up here you left earlier and earlier. Yeah," he continued, looking out into the night, "I'm surprised you've come up here again. Must be some special reason."

He fought the impulse to strike Lawrence with his fist. He wanted to leave but wanted more to set Lawrence straight. He was still sweating slightly from the arm-wrestling and the liquor and he did not much feel like telling Lawrence what his "special reason" was or arguing with him about the way a person ought to live. Lawrence had no right to say anything to him about these things.

"Stop acting like a goddamned nosy lawyer and poking your head into what isn't your business." He took the cigar from his mouth and laid it on the railing.

Lawrence glared at him. Apparently he had no intention of leaving the porch.

"Listen, maybe you didn't mean what you just said," Carlyle began, deciding to try a calmer approach. "Maybe you're just not used to drinking. I don't know. I'm going to go back inside before I stop excusing you and do something rash." But before he could move Lawrence started to shout.

"You're telling *me* I've had too much to drink? Yeah, I'm a goddamned nosy lawyer, all right, and I'm having some drinks. You're nothing but a run-down alcoholic who has to sell off his property to keep up with the tab!"

Stunned, Carlyle stepped back from the railing. Lawrence kept on shouting.

"Does your own wife get a new set of teeth? No! A new dress? Never! But *you* come up here and have a good old time with the boys! *Let* the goddamn hurricane hit! Leave her there alone! Who cares?"

Carlyle turned, to grab the man and try to shake some sense into him, but stopped when he saw Lawrence's face. Sweat was rolling off his high forehead, and he kept running his palm up over his forehead and into his hair. Even Lawrence's clothes were wrinkled, his usual uniform: dark suit, white shirt, narrow tie.

"You're thinking Helen's been crying to me. She hasn't. But I know what goes on, and I know her well enough to know how she feels. The thing that kills me is, she won't say a word against you, Carlyle Simpson, you bastard!"

"Who you calling a bastard?" He felt frozen, his right arm rigid.

"Don't tell me you've never threatened her. I know you've hit her, but she'd never talk about it. I know a lot about you, Carlyle. More than you know about yourself, maybe. It doesn't matter how. But let me ask you just one question. Why in God's name did you move to Florida? When all of Helen's roots were here, when she and the children didn't want to leave, when your own friends and family were here? What made you want to move to Florida?"

Lawrence's tone kept shifting, and there was no way to predict what he would say next or when he would finally shut up. Any other man saying these things would have felt the force of Carlyle's fist by now, but this was different from other insults he had struck out against in the past: this was standing on your own land and suddenly feeling the ground shift beneath you.

"Don't give me that shit you gave us back then about the climate," Lawrence said. "What was it, anyway?"

Lawrence was a skinny stick figure in clothes that were too loose for him, gripping the railing for support. Carlyle could find no words to shout back into the heavy, moist air that hung between them.

"Or did you know exactly what you were doing, committing an act of violence against your wife? It was cruel, what you did, Carlyle Simpson, it was cruel to Helen and to Bob and to Sarah. You had *no right* to take them away from Townsend. This was their home. They belonged to it as sure as you thought they belonged to you. You had no right to steal them away from it!" He paused, and his voice dropped, "Maybe it would have been different if you had known how to be a decent husband and father. Maybe then it wouldn't have mattered where you forced them to go."

Through his socks and shoes Carlyle sensed the firm concrete floor beneath him. "Shut up, Lawrence. You just shut up. What do you think I did, *kidnap* her?" He grabbed Lawrence by the shoulders and shook him. "She married me, didn't she? And no one hit her over the head and threw her into the trunk to take her to Florida either!"

Carlyle pushed him against the railing. Lawrence offered no resistance, but went on talking.

"You *knew* she didn't want to go, but you knew she would go. That's the most horrible of your crimes, the worst thing. You knew she *would*."

"Yeah. That's right," Carlyle said bitterly. He let Lawrence go. "No divorces for any Joneses. No scandals in the Jones family. You think she's so fuckin' wonderful, why haven't you just brought her on back up here for good?"

He felt as worn out as Lawrence looked. They both stood a moment, breathing heavily, until Lawrence walked back to the french doors, opened them quietly and left.

Carlyle looked at the railing; the cigar he had put there was gone. He hoped it had not fallen on one of the umbrellas over the tables, it might stain the vinyl or burn it. He lit another cigar, puffing blue rings of smoke over the invisible rolling hills of Townsend Country Club, until Pete came to ask if he was ready to leave.

FIVE

LEVEL, PLUMB, AND SQUARE

Nothing is ever plumb, level or square. —*Alan Dugan*

When he came home, Carlyle found that the hurricane had struck Florida after all. It had moved inland from the west coast and weakened gradually as it encountered the vertical resistance of trees and houses. Still, it had ripped limbs from trees, blown down wires, caused rivers to overflow and damaged bridges.

Duffy's boat was still sitting in the driveway but there was a dent wider than his fist in its side. He pulled himself stiffly out of the car. There was debris everywhere. Branches and palm fronds had fallen into the boat from the trees at the edge of the lot. But he couldn't see anything that might have caused the dent. For the first time his own lawn looked as unkempt as his neighbor's. The grass, watered by heavy rains, had grown as high as the tops of his socks.

Helen was not in the kitchen and was not sitting in the living room watching her afternoon soap operas, either. He found her in bed.

"Oh, is that you, Carlyle?"

She struggled to sit up and throw off the covers. He could not understand why she would need covers on this warm day. And Helen was not given to taking naps in the middle of the afternoon.

"Yeah. It's me. What's the matter, you sick or something?"

She stood up and wrapped her light blue nylon robe around her faded yellow housedress, something he did not remember seeing her do often. "Just a touch of cold, that's all. The electricity went out one night."

How could she catch cold from having no electricity in the summertime? The dampness and all that rain, that was it.

"Oh. The hurricane wasn't bad, was it?" He tried to sound unconcerned.

"No, it wasn't too bad here. The beaches were hit hard, though. Bob came over and stayed with me the night it hit. Are you hungry? Have you had lunch? I can fix you something."

"Naw, I'm not hungry now. I can wait till dinnertime." He watched her find her slippers and put them on. "Don't suppose you'd happen to know what hit Duffy's boat?"

"I didn't know anything had hit it."

"Got a dent in it bigger than my fist. Must have been a big rock or something."

"Where? I guess I didn't notice."

"Didn't you bother to check out the yard before the hurricane, make sure there wasn't anything that would fly around?" He tried to keep the anger out of his voice. She twirled one of her blue-grey curls absently on her fingers, an unconscious habit which infuriated him. "Shit, I guess I can't go off and leave for *one day* without somethin' going to pot around here." He turned and left the room, stomping as hard as he could on the carpet; she had better sense than to say anything, or at least anything he could hear. He wanted to go to Johnny's, but he would have to mow the grass first. He could not stand to see it looking as if no one cared about it.

At dinner she asked him about the trip.

"Sold the property for less than it's worth, but Pete's a good friend. Compromised at six an acre."

"So that's eighteen thousand, right?"

"Yes, that's eighteen thousand," he said flatly.

"How's Mavis?"

"Oh, she looked fine to me." He kept on eating. The food was greasy, but he was too tired to complain.

"And Billy?"

"Didn't see him."

"I thought you said you stayed with Pete and Mavis."

"I did. Didn't see Billy, that's all."

She waited. He kept on eating. Greasy macaroni and cheese, spoonbread, roast beef.

"Oh," she said finally, as though she realized she wasn't going to get anything out of him. "Well, who else did you see? I suppose you would have called if you had gone to visit Sarah."

He ignored what he heard in her voice. After a moment he told her about Ned Sorrell and the others at the club.

"Saw your brother Lawrence too, but Alice wasn't with him."

She waited. He looked at her to see whether she had heard from Lawrence after the club party, but he could not tell anything from her expression. He noticed that her skin was growing more wrinkled.

"Well, did you talk with Lawrence? How's the practice, or did he say?"

He looked down at his food, spearing a slab of greasy roast beef, cooked to a uniform brown like cardboard.

"Didn't ask him about that. We didn't talk about much of anything, nothing important. I don't think Alice is too good. Ask me, Lawrence didn't look too good either — nothing to get upset about," he quickly added. "He's probably just been worrying too much." *The way your family does.* He bit into the tough roast beef and watched her to see if she understood.

He went to bed early, taking the newspaper to the bedroom with him. Probably he should have waited until tomorrow to mow the lawn. He was much too tired. He undressed and lay down carefully in his own firm bed at last.

Here it was, already late summer, and Beaumont's house just begun. He reached the site early, while the air was still cool and moist, before the sun could burn off the dew covering grass and bushes and tree leaves. Soda cans and beer bottles and cigarette butts covered the cement flooring. Carlyle picked up the long handled push broom from where it lay and began to sweep, starting at the north edge of the concrete and guiding the broom slowly by its still wet handle without any jerks or stops, to the southern edge. He pushed the accumulated scraps, wood shavings, and sawdust off the floor. Then he turned and repeated the action, moving back toward the northern edge. He swept the entire concrete floor, scattered the sawdust on the lot surrounding the house. By the time he had finished the sun was up and drying out the world left soggy by the night.

Scovill, Scovill's son, and another carpenter came in to do the roof. The trusses had been set, southern yellow pine. Scovill and Johnson, the other framing carpenter, came in to put the lookouts on and run the subfascia around the building. Scovill had his son cutting pieces. Carlyle watched the three of them all morning, and when it was time for their noon break he drove to a convenience store and brought back sandwiches and beer. Scovill did not drink, but Johnson sat down with Carlyle on the concrete flooring and told him about the hurricane while the two of them sipped beer. Scovill and his boy had brought a small ice chest with soda pop, and they sat in Scovill's truck, keeping to themselves. Carlyle decided Johnson was all right, a little dumb maybe, but a good guy who would never make trouble.

"Yeah, I guess you were lucky the hurricane hit when it did, Mr. Simpson. Doesn't seem to have hurt anything. Good thing the roof wasn't started with the plywood and everything just sittin' there gettin' ruined by the rain." Johnson spoke like a man sitting back comfortably in a rocking chair, seeming oblivious to the hard floor under them. Carlyle envied Johnson, a man who could be at ease in any situation. He was short and stocky, like Carlyle, and a few years older than Scovill, for some reason not nearly as irritating as Scovill. Carlyle couldn't keep from wondering why Scovill refused the beer. Maybe he didn't want to drink in front of the kid. But no, that didn't make sense. The kid was old enough to have a beer.

He turned to Johnson.

"Yeah, I guess we were lucky. You know, that mason's work is all right. Did you notice?"

"Yeah, I noticed it looked like a real clean job."

"Better than a clean job. He did it like it's supposed to be done, took his time, and I can tell you this house is absolutely square. You won't find many of these slapped-together subdivision jobs that are perfectly square. I measured it. Not a fraction off. Makes your job a whole lot easier, too."

Johnson nodded and finished drinking his beer.

Carlyle wondered if Johnson understood the importance of what he was saying. If Johnson knew how often things were let go — things like level, plumb, and square: the things it took a good contractor and good men to make sure of. If the mason made the house too long even by half an inch, things would be irreparably out of square. Most people wouldn't even notice. But he would. Anyone who knew construction would. And the house would not be sound. The block had to be absolutely vertical, absolutely plumb, because if it tilted even one quarter of an inch, the house would be off. All kinds of problems could result, not only with doors that wouldn't fit. The mason had done a good job, but if the carpenters didn't do the interior walls right the house could still go out of square. He wanted Scovill and Johnson to know he would be right behind them, checking.

The next day Scovill and Johnson took staple guns and began to sheet the roof with plywood, stapling the sheets together with aluminum clips. Carlyle had had Helen call Bob the night before, and he sent Bob on errands — to get more nails and lumber and felt paper, and to talk to the roof man Carlyle wanted, to see if he could come in later in the week.

The sun was unbearably hot. It was still early, but Carlyle had already removed his sport shirt, and his white undershirt was nearly soaked through. Neither of the two men on the roof wore hats; Carlyle wondered how they could stand it without something to shield their eyes. He didn't mind working in the hot sun, but he had to have his hat on when he did. Scovill removed his T-shirt, and Carlyle was surprised to see that his entire torso was almost as dark as his arms. The Scovill kid helped with ladders and materials, but didn't do the sheeting. He was careful to stay out of Carlyle's way, but he was clearly aware that the old fogey was keeping an eye on his daddy up there on the roof.

It seemed to Carlyle that Scovill had begun to change his pace and was going too fast. Johnson moved more slowly. He seemed to be taking careful aim with the gun, but Carlyle could not tell, from where he stood below them, whether Johnson was shooting right either. He shouted to Scovill to slow down. Scovill looked at him and grunted, but kept working, perhaps imperceptibly slower. Carlyle went to the ladder and had the kid hold it for him. He struggled up to the roof to look at the clips. Aluminum clips could hold better than nails, *if* they were shot right, but if not, they were nearly worthless. He crawled slowly along the roof to inspect the staples Scovill and Johnson had shot so far.

"Hey, slow down. Look at what you're doing here. These things have got to go in straight or not at all." Johnson stopped immediately, poised on the roof like a trusting animal. Scovill shot two more clips and then, still on hands and knees, glared at Carlyle. The three of them posed there, on trusses and plywood, resting on all fours. "Might as well go back to using nails, you don't staple right," Carlyle said.

Scovill took a cigarette from his pack on the plywood near him, and lit it iwith a lighter he took from his jeans pocket, still crouching like a lean lion. Johnson watched, puzzled. Scovill was closest to Carlyle, so Carlyle asked for Scovill's gun.

"Old man like you hadn't oughta be up here on an unfinished roof," he muttered, but he threw the staple gun. Carlyle caught it. The metal was hot from the sun. He motioned for Scovill to move closer, and on the nearest sheet of plywood he began to use the gun, even though he wasn't sure he would be able to handle it exactly the way he knew it had to be handled. All he knew was that the clips had to go in the wood perfectly straight, and some of the clips already in the plywood sheets were carelessly placed.

He showed Scovill the way he wanted it done, looking not at the man but at the plywood and the gun. The metal felt pleasantly warm and smooth in his hand, like a semi-precious stone. He shot the clips slowly, carefully, finishing a sheet of plywood, and waiting for Scovill to take notice. Johnson, too, had watched carefully. Carlyle could tell, when he looked at the men's faces, that they had seen what he wanted them to see. He put the gun down and backed slowly down the ladder.

"Now, I don't mean slow down like a couple of old ladies. You can get the job done today and still do it right. You ought to be faster than me." *Old man.* Some old man he was. Scovill had said it only out of spite, and Carlyle sensed that the man probably wished he hadn't, or saw that he was wrong. He hated working with men like Scovill who had to be shown how to do things and hated you for showing them.

That afternoon he stopped by Johnny's on his way home, hoping to catch Nelson after work. He felt gritty all over and much too warm.

The regulars were talking about him, he could tell.

"Well, there he is, the man with the sixth sense. He knew that damned hurricane was going to hit, so he just hightailed it out of here for awhile. Now it's over, he's back. Ain't that right, Carly?"

Before he could say anything, everyone was telling him to sit down and have a drink. They talked about the damage the hurricane had done. Carlyle did not mention Duffy's boat. It nagged at him, scratching around in the back of his mind like some old, dirty fisherman digging in a bait bin. He was glad to find Nelson at the table.

"Good thing you got back in time for the match," Nelson said. "Guess you don't need any practice, though."

Carlyle put his arm up on the table. "Guess I do. Wrestled an old buddy up in Carolina and he beat me." The match would be coming up in less than two weeks, and he couldn't let them lose money on him.

They wrestled. Nelson struggled with about three-quarters of his best strength, and Carlyle beat him.

"You can do better than that. What's the matter with you?"

Nelson pretended he had given his all. "How old is that old buddy of yours?"

"Older'n you."

"Well, maybe he lifts weights," Nelson said, rubbing his biceps. "You know, Carlyle, there's some of the guys might be coming in that day who *do* lift weights. You ever thought about that?"

"Listen, Nelson, I ain't got time for that nonsense. If men today don't *work* and build their muscles that way, I guess they got nothing better to do than to pay good money just to make big muscles for the girls."

"Or each other," Nelson grinned.

"Shut up, Nelson," someone said.

"Let 'em go to some fancy air-conditioned place with carpets and a whirlpool bath," Carlyle continued, ignoring the interruption. "Ain't fit to go out and do an honest day's work; that's the place for 'em." He knew Nelson would know what he meant. Nelson was from Miami; he had told Carlyle once that he had seen enough Cubans and Jews and lazy white people to last him a lifetime.

"I'm a little worried, Carly. We don't know who might show up, or how many. What if a lot of guys we don't know come in?"

"Who's going to show up? You and all the guys from the trailer park and a few of Johnny's friends and maybe a few guys who see the sign. Johnny said he'd put it on the sign."

"Yeah, and the guys who see the sign are the ones we might be thinking about."

They stared at each other.

"All right. I know your wife's been telling you she don't like the company you keep, but you're going to have to stay here and wrestle some more," Carlyle said. They locked arms. "And put something *into* it this time, huh?"

At home, after dinner, he stood in the driveway frowning at Duffy's boat and looking at the sky for hints of rain. If it were to rain during the night, the plywood sheeting could be damaged and they would probably have to do it over. He could usually tell when it was going to rain. There would be a smell in the air, the humidity rising, gathering up all the moisture from leaves, from houses, from the asphalt streets and the cement sidewalks. And if it rained tonight, the plywood would soak it up and warp. He could imagine the smell of the soggy wood, could see in his mind the dark stain spreading across the tan sheets. But no, it would not rain, not tonight. And then tomorrow he would have them all there, Bob and Johnson and Scovill and the kid, and they would put the felt paper on, before it could rain on the plywood, before the joints could swell or the wood could warp. They were behind schedule, but the house would be finished before Beaumont could find a buyer for the old one.

He noticed the dent in Duffy's boat again, like an old scar he had forgotten until it started to itch. He didn't like it; he couldn't leave the boat there looking like that. He hated to see things looking broken down and neglected; it said something about a person when he didn't keep things up. If you had a boat you took care of it, or you did not bother to have a boat at all. A dent like that couldn't be covered up. You couldn't hide it. You would have to work hard to get rid of it, then repaint and seal the whole boat, and even then you'd always know in the back of your mind, yes, it looks nice, but that boat has been dented; yes, it looks nice, but this isn't the original finish. And that would mean something.

He could not leave the boat sitting there in his driveway with that dent in it, but he did not have time to take it down and have it worked on, either. Not tomorrow. And then he had already contacted the roofing contractor to come out and shingle the roof at the end of the week. Three days at least before he could be free to worry with Duffy's boat. Sure, he could take it in tomorrow. Or the next day. Hire men to do work on a house, then go off and leave them alone to do it. But he knew better. He would be there every day the men worked, watching them, making sure they did not make mistakes and then keep right on so no one would notice. The mistakes would still be there, and even if no one else spotted them, *he* would spot them, sooner or later. Something would show up, only it would be too late, and he would know, even if no one else knew, that Beaumont was getting a flawed house.

But the house would not be flawed. He spat on the grass at the edge of the driveway, getting rid of the taste of tobacco from his last cigar. The house would not be flawed because he would be there to keep an eye on those men, every day. It was right so far, and it would stay right. It was level, plumb and square, and he would see that the rest of the house down to the last stroke of the paintbrush would do justice to the foundation and the roof. He would leave Duffy's boat, much as it pained him, for the next three days, maybe the next week, maybe the next month. He turned and walked up the driveway into the garage, with the taste of tobacco still in his dry mouth.

"Lucky it didn't rain last night," Bob said nervously. He was like a newcomer in town trying to strike up a conversation with the tough-looking locals, hoping he wouldn't look like a sissy. Yes, nervous. Carlyle didn't like that but he had no complaint about the boy's work. Watching him help Scovill and Johnson put the felt paper over the plywood sheeting on the roof, Carlyle decided he wasn't sorry he had offered Bob the job. He did his work, and he had to admit that nervous as he was, Bob was not as sorry a case as Scovill's son, who was busy running around, always asking could he do something, get something, help out with this, with that—half of the time questions he didn't need to ask if he'd only look and see that his help wasn't needed, and he would be told what he should do and when he should do it.

"Well, that hurricane dumped enough rain on things to last a while," Carlyle said to Bob, thinking he ought to tell both of these kids just to calm down and do as they were told. Worrying was one of Helen's habits; so was nervousness, and it poked at him like a splinter whenever he saw it in Bob. He said nothing more but stood, first watching the men on the roof, then concentrating on the supplies stacked on the lot near the house. He examined the simplex nails with their extra large heads. Felt paper had to be laid down with simplex nails, and it didn't take much strength to drive a simplex nail solidly into plywood. He took a few of the nails in his hand, enjoying their smooth, cylindrical shape. Drive a nail through felt paper and plywood; drive it hard, and know it was fixed, secure. Like a finished house.

He left the site to order the blue-end studs for the frame; it was Scovill's job, but he wanted to be sure it was done. He stopped and bought a six pack of beer and some sandwiches. He tried to think of what Bob would eat. Was it ham or turkey the boy had liked? He remembered seeing Bob devour ham and mustard sandwiches when he was young, but that was years ago. Why couldn't he picture what his own son ate now, why couldn't he remember what he surely must have seen a hundred times and more at lunch, at dinner? What did the kid like to eat? He simply could not remember, and that irritated him. There had been the kitchen table and a kid there, or two kids, and then there were no kids at the table, and he could not remember ever seeing what the kids *ate*; they were often huddled, the two of them together or Bob or Sarah alone, huddled at a kind of distance from him, watchng him eat his steak. He decided to buy ham for Bob; all the men he had ever worked with had liked ham.

When he returned to the site, they ate lunch, Scovill and the kid again sitting in their truck with the doors and windows open, the kid's legs dangling over the edge of the seat, half outside the cab. Carlyle sat with Johnson and Bob on the cool concrete under the roof, drinking a beer and belching unashamedly.

"You know what we *oughta* have, go with this beer, is some good fresh grouper. Fried grouper and beer. Yum," Johnson said, biting into a sandwich.

"Yeah, fish and beer," Carlyle agreed. "Like to catch me some

red snapper one of these days and broil it. Don't need anything else
but snapper; that's a good meal."

"Have you taken the boat out yet, Pop?" Bob asked.

"Haven't had time, with all this—" he moved his arm, holding
the beer carefully, to indicate the house and the lot—"this big
headache, I guess you have to call it." He grinned and finished the
beer; how good and cold it was, and how easy it was, just to sit here
in the shade and drink beer and eat a crummy ham sandwich. He
didn't want to think about Duffy's boat, but there it was, spoiling
the cold beer. "You know that boat has a dent in it? I'll have to take
it in to see if Boatcraft can do anything with it."

"It wasn't dented before, was it?"

"No. I don't know what did it. I thought maybe the hurricane
had knocked somethin' up against it, but I couldn't find anything
that could have done it. Some *kid*, I guess. Took a rock or a hammer
to it."

Bob did not say anything, and Johnson stood up and stretched,
then slowly walked away.

"Damn kids. Just tear it up, tear it up, all they know how to do."

He sat with a sour taste in his mouth and watched Bob walk over
to the portable toilet. His second beer did not taste good to him. He
finished it, watching Scovill and Johnson scramble up the ladder,
with Bob behind them, to finish the roof papering.

When the men ran out of simplex nails, Scovill called down to
the kid, who was playing around with the lumber, collecting scraps
of discarded felt paper, hungry for things to do.

"I'll go down and get them," Bob said to Scovill.

But the kid was already off, picking up three boxes of nails from
the stack near the felt paper, trying to balance them in one hand as
he ran for the ladder. He was already climbing it, ignoring Bob's
protest, before anyone noticed that the ladder was not steady.
Carlyle was going over his list of supplies, when he saw the kid on
the ladder, and yelled at him for running with the nails. The kid ran
up too fast and when he missed a step, he caught himself by pulling
on the ladder. Carlyle watched in the searing heat for what seemed
an interminable moment: the ladder wobbled like an old lady in
high heels, then fell, almost gracefully, depositing young Scovill on

the ground with a soft thud, as if a bag of wet dirt had struck the dry soil.

Scovill was at the edge of the roof, staring down at the kid, who was lying on the ground, moaning, with the lopsided, big-headed nails scattered around him. Bob ran after Scovill to the roof's edge, hung back for a second, as if deciding whether to ask Carlyle to pick up the ladder, and then jumped. Carlyle watched his own son as he went through the air, detached momentarily from earth and house and everything firm. Amazingly, Bob landed on his feet like a cat, unhurt. He hurried over to the Scovill kid, helped Carlyle get the ladder off him, and checked his pulse. Bob asked the kid how he felt, where it hurt.

"Bring me that damned ladder!" Scovill screamed, and reluctantly Carlyle put the ladder back up, making sure it was steady this time. Scovill scrambled down, glaring at Carlyle, and as soon as he was standing on the ground face to face with him, said, "If that boy's hurt bad I'm gonna sue your ass, mister!"

Scovill stood there as if he were one of the pieces of sheeting that had just been stapled; his feet were riveted to the ground, but his body was tense, and Carlyle could see him breathing: drawing air in, drawing it in with a violence Carlyle knew intimately. Men breathed like that when they were using every bit of nerve they had to keep from striking out. Carlyle was about to tell Scovill it was the kid's own fault when Bob interrupted, shouting, "Well, don't just *stand* there! Somebody go find a phone and call an ambulance!"

Scovill sprang crazily from the spot and ran down the street toward the nearest house. Carlyle could not help thinking that Scovill was lucky to be working here rather than in that new subdivision. Beaumont had bought one of the last vacant lots left in this older neighborhood, a real neighborhood, where people had lived for many years. Scovill would find people here, and help for the kid; he wouldn't have to drive around looking for a pay phone.

"Here, give me your shirt," Bob said. Carlyle noticed that Bob had already removed his own shirt and put it over the boy. "We've got to keep him warm." Carlyle did not ask Bob why, in weather like this, anyone had to worry about keeping someone warm. He did as he was told, removing his sport shirt, which was still dry, and leaving his sweat-soaked undershirt on. But he moved mechanically; everything was happening too fast. Bob had taken control, keeping a clear head and using his knowledge of first aid from a course he had taken at the junior college. Johnson came down from the roof with his shirt too. By the time Scovill came back up the street, they could hear the approaching siren. Bob stayed with the boy (who, Carlyle had to remind himself, was not much younger than Bob) and explained to the medics what had happened. They talked with Bob as though he were their colleague. As the ambulance moved off, its siren beginning again, Carlyle wondered how much money this little mishap, a boy's carelessness, would cost him.

Johnson kept looking from Carlyle to Bob and back again.

"Well, I don't think it's too serious," Bob said. "It seemed more like shock than anything else. But you never know."

"Yeah. You never know," Carlyle said grimly.

They stood there for a while in awkward silence. Carlyle went to pick up his shirt and began to gather up the scattered nails. He filled one box and then took it up the ladder with him. It was too early to quit. He did not look back to see, but after a few minutes he heard the others following him. The three of them worked silently and finished papering the roof.

As they were leaving, Carlyle and Johnson watched Bob go to his old red jalopy with rusted sides. Johnson turned to Carlyle and said, "That's some kid you've got there."

Carlyle nodded.

Later that evening he sat at his desk in the little room just off the dining room. At least they had been able to dry-in the roof; he was relieved about that. The two roofing men were coming in to start shingling in the morning. It would probably take them two days, and then it would be time to begin building out the interior walls. He disliked Scovill, but he hoped Scovill's kid would be all right.

He could not seem to make himself comfortable in the straight-backed desk chair, or concentrate on the stacks of bills and the open checkbook in front of him. With the door to the dining room closed, it was so quiet he could not hear the television in the family room.

He picked up the telephone extension and held the receiver in one hand as he looked up the hospital number in the directory. Careful to keep his voice down, he called and asked about the younger Mr. Rodney Scovill, they said he had been released from the hospital only two hours after he had been admitted.

So the boy was all right; Carlyle wondered why he wasn't more relieved, why he still felt uneasy. Even though the boy might be all right, even though it was nobody's fault, really, in the first place, Scovill was spiteful enough to walk off and leave the job if he felt like it. Or botch it. That was more likely. There was no reason for Scovill to sue him, but Scovill was neither trustworthy nor predictable. He would be glad when it was all over, when the house was completed and he would never have to work with Scovill again. It seemed that the house itself held surprises; Carlyle had felt uneasy ever since he had found that Ben Starritt was no longer working, ever since he had handed Scovill the contract.

He was vaguely aware of time passing and of the fact that he had been unable to concentrate. He sat at his desk, alone, uneasy, and could barely remember any of the events of the day but this, the one event that could make all the difference in his schedule, in whether the house would be finished in time for Beaumont to move in before October. He remembered taking a few bites of some nameless, tasteless meat at dinner, while Helen asked him why he wasn't eating. As if he knew. He hated questions like that, and he didn't feel obliged to answer.

The checkbook was open before him; he had been intending to pay some bills. The check was a clear, unblemished blue like the blue of Duffy's boat without the marks, the few scratches, and the dent. It was blue as a lake, the way lakes are blue only in children's picture books; he remembered one, the book about the little girl who lived on a farm, the one he used to read sometimes to Sarah when she was little. She had heard that story over and over again and looked at it over and over again and she had ruined it with her crayons. Kids seemed to destroy everything sooner or later; they didn't know any better. The scarred-up furniture, marked walls, broken toys and vases and dishes: he had bought and paid for all of it and they had scratched it up, torn it up like little animals. They did things and then tried to hide what they had done. They learned dishonesty from the first, from their parents maybe, from each other. And now he sat at a scratched-up desk worrying about it years later, long after Bob and Sarah had forgotten all about it. And what about the kids who had made the dent, deliberately, in the blue boat? Would they forget all about that, years later?

He tore open the small envelopes before him, arranged all the bills in a stack and began to write checks. There was a fine layer of dust on the metal shade of his desk lamp. He ran his finger across the metal above the fluorescent tube. He did not write "filth" on it as he sometimes did.

He heard Helen walking slowly from the kitchen to his workroom. He gritted his teeth and waited for her to open the door.

"Don't you need more light in here?" She snapped on the overhead before he could answer.

He held a bill from her doctor, a pale yellow printed form, crisp and still smelling of the chemical that made multiple copies without the mess of carbon paper. The customer could pay the outrageous inflated fees without dirtying his hands. And the fee no doubt included an increase to pay for the fancy treated paper. He tried to remember whether Helen had said anything about a visit to the doctor. Yes; she had been quiet about it but Bob had taken her one day. That was supposed to be just for a check-up. This bill was for nearly a hundred dollars.

He sensed her hovering behind him, curious. She did not ask, but he told her. "Just paying some bills. Here's one from Dr. James, ninety-seven dollars. What was that for?" He turned to face her.

Her face flushed. "Oh, was it that much?"

"Yeah, it was that much," he said wearily. "That wasn't just a check-up, was it?"

"Well, he wanted to run some tests," she said.

"What kind of tests?" He folded his arms across his chest. She was making him ask questions he shouldn't have to ask, making him draw out every little piece of information just to find out what the doctor did. He had to wait for her to answer each simple question as if she were speaking to a slow child. Well, he was *not* a slow child; he was smarter than any of her college friends and she had often agreed that that was true. But her own slowness was infuriating. She stood with her arms crossed below her sagging breasts, her faded print housedress loose around her, her reluctant hands hugging her elbows. He watched her gathering and rejecting words in her mind; he could tell from her posture and from her creased forehead that she was worried, that she knew something he might not like and that she was afraid he might not like it, and might show her that he did not like it. He knew all this as she gathered the sentences she finally spoke.

"Had to check my overall health. Blood, urine, cardiogram . . ." She looked as though she were trying to think of more of them. "I guess that was it."

"So you had all those tests and what did they find?" He became aware that he was pressing his teeth together — not actually gritting them yet in anger. He felt as though he had been put onto a treadmill: it had started now, the anger, and he could not help the inevitable direction it would take, his blood coursing fast and hot, his hard, fast breathing.

She noticed it too, his breathing. Maybe she had noticed a change in his voice which he had not intended. It seemed to happen without his will.

"Well, it's not much. Some anemia is all, I guess. So I'm taking iron. I was feeling weak and tired, and he wanted to do the tests to rule out anything serious."

"So you spend a hundred bucks for him to tell you to take Geritol! It's only money. Who cares?"

Doctors always ran too many tests, any time they thought they could get away with it. They were just after the money. Carlyle suddenly felt very tired. He had said all this to Helen it seemed thousands of times over the years. She had taken the kids to the doctor too often, yearly check-ups for no reason, and every time the bills had to be paid just the same. She had wanted to take them to the dentist for check-ups, too, but he had forbidden that, and both kids had grown up just as he had, with the teeth God gave them. If you took care of your teeth they'd last a lifetime; though his own were grey and sometimes painful, he had no real complaints. By the time you were his age, you couldn't expect teeth to be pretty. As long as he could still eat, what did it matter? Helen knew better than to try to get him to pay dentists, but every time she thought she had a little pain, off she would go to the doctor and expect Carlyle to pay for it. His insurance would pay for most of it, but it was the principle of the thing that irritated him. Throwing money away.

"I'm not taking Geritol," Helen said. "It's a prescription."

She seemed to think that "prescription" was some magic word that would justify everything. Her respect for doctors and for liberal politicians was like a superstition; nothing you could do or say would remove it. Prescription. As if that meant anything. It was just a label to hide behind. Sell you ferrous sulphate and call it a prescription when you could have bought it at the grocery store, in vitamins or Geritol, and everybody *knew* what was in Geritol, so if people bought it, it was their own damn fault. Helen wouldn't take vitamins; she wouldn't take Geritol, either, but she'd swear by her aspirin for arthritis and by her prescriptions, whatever they were for, because the *doctor* approved them. She didn't have many prescriptions, but you might as well not even *ask* why she took the ones she did. He felt like telling her that she didn't need a damned doctor to put her on machines just to tell her she was getting fat and old and a damn sight weaker than she used to be. Wasn't any doctor could tell her a way out of that, not with all the diets and prescriptions and machines.

"Well, you just go on," he said bitterly. "Here I got all kinds of expenses and worries and an accident at the site and maybe no carpenter, and *you* go out to the damned doctor for a social call that costs me nearly a hundred bucks!"

He opened and slammed a desk drawer, then another, and another, as hard as he could.

"You didn't tell me there was an accident—" she said, but he kept on opening and slamming drawers. She stopped and retreated to the other part of the house, leaving him with the doctor bills and the accident, alone in a room, in a house that he had once proudly built and boasted was the finest in the neighborhood, a house that he had never imagined he could hate so much.

SIX

JOHNNY'S BUCKET

Sure enough, Scovill did not show. In the days since the accident, the roof had been finished. The two men who came out to do it had worked silently and efficiently and done it in two days. Carlyle had watched them the first day, until he was convinced of their competence. Then he left them alone long enough to take Duffy's boat over to Boatcraft, to be repaired. Boatcraft built new Fiberglas boats and cabin cruisers, but they also did repairs on all kinds of older boats. They couldn't give him a date for completion of the work. He had expected as much: it was a small job, hardly worth their time. "It might be weeks," the supervisor had told him, "but you never know. We'll get to it when we can." They would call him. "Looks like an easy surface job. Shouldn't take too long," the man had said. "What happened, anyway? Somebody take a hammer to it?"

He had not known what to say, and felt embarrassed to find that his own worst suspicions might be true. Although he had reached the conclusion himself that vandals had done the damage, he had half hoped that the people at Boatcraft would tell him something else. Surely the hurricane could have heaved up a big rock, a branch—but no, he knew a branch could not have done it. A rock, yes. But rocks could be thrown by people as well as by hurricanes, and there had been no rock in the driveway or the front yard that could have produced that dent. Had someone thrown it, then? Pitched a rock at the unglamorous blue paint, then picked up the weapon and carried it away? He had sensed that, had known that, but having his suspicion confirmed made him question it again. Who would do such a thing? Teenagers of course—scattered, one here, one there, down the blocks in the neighborhood.

He had gone back to the site to get away from this bitter obsession that had its hooks in him. He did not want to think about it or to feel what he knew he would feel, or to do what he knew he would do if he thought too long about it. He had returned to the site not because he had to oversee the roof men, but because he needed to be at the site, where he would not think about anything but the work, about anything but the house. The work—unashamedly hard, sweaty work in the clear, unsparing sun. That was healthy, it would drive out the shadows that tried to catch at his sleeve and pull him into their darkness. He had visited that place; he knew people who liked to live there—Helen sometimes, and her family, and too many men in construction and business and government. They wanted to live in places where nothing would stand, where every house was built on a swamp and had cracks in its foundation. They lived with meaningless dreams, idle speculation, hopeless worries. Helen could live there, and all those who did not want or need to stand up and work in the sunlight.

He watched the roof men for two days, sensing a change, a dryness in the middle of the humid hot summer, even as his clothes stuck to him and he mopped his forehead. He felt a crack spreading: somewhere, some dirty grey crack was pushing everything solid away.

He waited until nine-thirty on the day the roof was finished, the day when Scovill was supposed to come, and then he called Scovill. Johnson stood looking nervous, without his usual easygoing smile. His eyes darted like Scovill's as the hour grew late. After a while, as Carlyle paid little attention, Johnson began to pick through the lumber that had been delivered the day before and that Carlyle had not bothered to look at or cull. Johnson went about slowly selecting two-by-fours for the framing, the interior walls. Without saying anything, Carlyle went to his car and drove home to phone.

"Scovill? This is Simpson. Hope your boy is all right. They told me at the hospital that they released him the same day you took him in." He hated having to be polite. Scovill and he both knew how they felt about each other, but he did not want to say anything that would push Scovill over the fine line—if it had not already been crossed.

"You didn't call to check up on my son," Scovill said bluntly. Carlyle's blood ran cold.

"Well, I *was* wondering why you're not at the site. We need you to do the interior walls. You know that. Johnson's there."

"Well, I'm not. So that's clear. I've got to take my son to a specialist today to see if we can find out what's wrong with him. He doesn't move right since that fall."

"But I thought they released him because he was all right."

"Sure — they set the arm and didn't find anything else just then. But his other arm doesn't move right, and he's got a limp. So we're going to find out what it is. Nerve damage or what. And I'm not coming to work today, and I may not come in again until I know what's wrong with my son."

"But you have a contract," Carlyle began.

"Screw the damned contract! You don't understand *anything*, do you, mister? I'm talking about my *son*!"

Carlyle paused, unsure how to proceed; Scovill was irrational, unpredictable. His anger seemed disproportionate. Carlyle was not used to trying to calm other people, and this time it wasn't Helen's hysteria, which he could ignore, or a disgruntled laborer he could easily get rid of.

It was Scovill, an inferior carpenter who was unfortunately the best one around, and more important, the carpenter Carlyle had hired; if he had to change carpenters now, the work would be delayed. Johnson was slow; it would take him at least four days to do this part of the job if he had to work alone. And they were already behind schedule because of the hurricane. He was sitting at his own desk, but he did not feel comfortable in his chair. What do you say to appease a man you don't like?

"All right, don't worry about the contract," he told Scovill. "Listen, can't your wife take him to the doctor, so you could come on to work?"

"My wife works," Scovill said curtly. "She can't take time off. When my boy needs to go somewhere, either I let him borrow the truck or I take him. Maybe he hasn't grown up as fast as other kids. I don't know. But my boy knows that if he needs to see a doctor, I'll take him. I'm not going to let him go by himself."

Carlyle could hear some commotion at the other end; evidently the boy was saying something in the background. Scovill turned his head aside to answer. "No. Not until *I* say so. You may *think* you're fine, but we've got to be sure. I'm not letting you drive with your arm like that." Then his voice came loud and sharp again into the mouthpiece. "Listen, Mr. Simpson, you've got Johnson. You're just gonna have to wait. If you want to get another carpenter, go right ahead."

Carlyle heard the boy's muffled protests again.

"All right, Scovill, now look here. I don't want to have to look for another man, and I don't want to lose any more time than I have to. If today's out, all right. But couldn't you take the boy to the doctor and see that he's all right and still come on out and do the job tomorrow?"

He had said it, much as he disliked saying it. It was as far as he would go. He was surprised to find himself actually afraid of losing Scovill He kept thinking of Johnson and what the extra days would mean. Finding a man he liked wouldn't be easy; finding any sort of decent carpenter with free time would be nearly impossible. He waited. There were muffled arguments again.

"All right," Scovill said slowly into the mouthpiece. "If I can find anything out today, maybe I'll come in tomorrow and help Johnson finish the job. It will depend on how I feel about it after we see the specialist. If I'm going to come in, I'll be there early."

It was a disgrace for a man like Carlyle Simpson, the builder, to have to listen to such arrogance from a bastard like Scovill. There were Scovills everywhere—cocky bastards who resented anyone who knew more than they did, anyone who had earned respect. That was it. They refused to respect authority. It irked Carlyle that this man whom he did not respect refused to respect him.

After he hung up the phone, Helen came into the room, asking would he be staying home, would he want his lunch at home, would he please tell her what had happened, what kind of accident had he mentioned the other night, and was anyone hurt, and who, and how badly, and was Bob there, and what was going to happen to the schedule? She said Harold Beaumont had called that morning and asked.

Oh, he had, had he? Harold Beaumont had called to ask about the accident and the schedule because some big mouth had told him about it. Who? Had Scovill gone ahead and called the man up and told him some trash? Carlyle felt himself redden with anger. They'd slit your throat if they had the chance.

"So Beaumont's pissed," he said. Helen flinched. She was offended by foul language except for her own mealy-mouthed expressions, like "hell's bells."

"No, wait a minute, Carlyle. He just *asked*. What *did* happen, anyway? You've got insurance if anyone was hurt, don't you? *Was* somebody badly hurt?"

"No, nobody was hurt, dammit! Scovill's kid got on a wobbly ladder and fell and that's all that happened. It was his own damn fault and he got a broken arm and there probably isn't a single other thing wrong with him, except that Scovill's gonna try to *make* something be wrong with him just to get at me!" He ignored her comments and went on, feeling hot and seeing, he thought, with greater clarity than he had ever perceived what, in fact, was happening to him. "They're trying to make a fool out of me because they thought they got rid of Simpson ten years back and now they're just waiting to see him fall on his face. Well, he ain't going to, I can tell 'em that for sure. I got dumb slow Johnson out there now, probably take him four or five days, but he can do it if he has to."

Helen did not retreat as he had expected; she pulled up a chair from the corner and sat facing him at his desk.

"Now wait. What makes you think anybody's planning to "get" you? Carlyle, you can't start worrying like this. You did that before, remember?"

Before you quit, she meant. The muscles in his face tightened, his lips drew together.

"But you *do* remember, don't you, Carlyle? You know you can't afford to get like that again. Your health —"

"There's not a damn thing wrong with my health!" he thundered. "And don't *you* start telling me what I can and can't do, you old meddling *bitch!*"

He saw it strike her, the word that could probably hurt her most. She recoiled as if from a whiplash, her face stricken like the wizened, worn face of her own mother. And suddenly he felt small and worn himself, and, watching her crumpled face, could taste his own poison as it entered him.

She left the room, hunched, shaking, unable to speak. And he felt very dry, very thirsty. There was sourness in his mouth, as if he had drunk nothing for days.

All afternoon he wrestled, free at last of words and the meanings behind them. This was the place he had to come to at last, the only place where he could relax without anger. He carried the anger and hatred around with him like a rough-edged cinder block; it chafed against his skin, and he could not find any place to set it down. Except at Johnny's, where the smooth glass door separated the cool, dark interior from the painful glare and the relentless humid heat. He would enter and leave the anger waiting for him outside. He would not be free of it for long.

He made short work of a couple of retirees from the trailer park; when some younger men came in later, he bought a pitcher of beer and persuaded them to wrestle too. His right arm was red, and the skin was stretched over the blood-swelled veins like a bedspread over a carelessly made bed. His grip on the young man's hand was hard and sure. They knew he meant business; no one needed words. He could let his arm speak for him; his own mute strength was enough here. Nowhere else could he relax and enjoy himself without needing words for everything. When he wrestled a man, and other men watched, they could talk to each other, but he did not have to talk to them if he did not want to.

The two young men did not talk much as Carlyle drove their arms down and forced them flat onto the formica. He brought their arms down twice each and satisfied himself that he could do well enough, even with the younger ones, in the match tomorrow. The two young men shook their heads at each other, thanked him for the beer, and moved to the pool table at the other end of the room.

Johnny, who was young enough himself to run the bar and run around with half the barmaids, came over to his table. Vicki, who Carlyle was reasonably certain was *not* running around with Johnny, brought them each a beer.

"On the house, Johnny says." She winked at Carlyle before she went back to the bar.

Johnny sat down and took one of the beers. His skin was very dark; a natural olive color. It didn't matter that he was inside, in this dark place, most of the time. He always looked healthy and tanned. If you met him on the street you would not be able to guess his occupation. Carlyle liked Johnny all right; the bar was run efficiently; the service, the sandwiches, and the drinks, from the cold draught beer to the house scotch, were always good. Carlyle liked the dark room because you could always find a seat at the bar or a regular chair at a table. Even though the air was stale from cigarette smoke, he felt he could breathe here.

"Hey, Carly, did you see the sign? I got it on the sign out there — come in tomorrow at eight o'clock to challenge the arm-wrestling champion," Johnny said.

He had not noticed the sign, but he nodded.

"I saw you practicing with those two over there —" Johnny nodded in the direction of the pool table. "So I guess you haven't forgotten how."

"No way. I'll be here; you can count on it. What've you got in the bucket so far?"

Johnny collected all the bets in a tin pail without acknowledging that betting was going on. The men came in, wrote their first names, the amount of the bet and the name of their choice for winner on a slip of paper and put it in the bucket. Anyone who wanted to wrestle would put five dollars in the bucket, with his own name. Then he could bet on himself, and his friends could bet on him. If anyone beat Carlyle, the winner would get the five dollars back, plus half of all the bets placed on Carlyle. If no one could beat Carlyle, the men who bet on him would keep their money, and the money bet against Carlyle would be divided among them.

"Got ten slips down on you already, and just two guys who say they'll wrestle you," Johnny told him. "I'm not telling you who. You can go look in the bucket yourself if you're so damned nervous about it."

"Why should I be nervous?" He raised his arm and set his elbow on the table, his palm open.

Johnny leaned back in his chair. He shook his head, and waved his hand back and forth.

"No way I'm wrestlin' you."

"Well, tell me how much is riding on these two guys."

Reluctantly, Johnny said, "Got themselves and a couple of friends betting on them. Oh, I don't know, maybe sixty or seventy bucks. Of course, most of it will come in tomorrow. After a few drinks, they'll start putting the money down. Just you try to keep it goin', huh?"

"You said you'd import some residents from the nursing home, didn't you? I reckon I can beat *them* all right . . . Well, I'm an old geezer, I guess, but I think I can still beat these guys in the trailer parks and most of the younger guys too. Let 'em come on. I'm not scared of a few grunts with big arms. There's a little more to wrestling than lifting weights and busting out your shirts."

Johnny looked at him steadily, as if he were trying to see something hidden in Carlyle's face.

"What is it, anyway? Just confidence? Or is it some secret?"

He took a swig of beer. "Keeps me goin'? Maybe that's it. Or maybe it's concentration."

He would not allow just anyone to push his arm down, not when he wanted to keep it upright. When Pete did it—and that had bothered him, no question about it—he had not been concentrating. When he concentrated, when he wanted to keep his arm upright, he could resist any man who wanted to move it down. Maybe it was a secret, that power of concentration.

He went back to the site where Johnson was still working at his slow pace, holding the long pieces of lumber in straight perpendicular to the floor and nailing the studs in place. Carlyle watched Johnson nailing the studs. He tried to count the number of nails the carpenter was using on each piece. As the hot sun beat down on him, he realized that he had had one or two beers too many that afternoon. It was pleasant, standing in the sun, a little sleepy, a little drunk. But it was hard to count the nails. If a carpenter didn't use enough nails on each stud, the framing would not be solid. He had seen too many carpenters rush through jobs. Each point of stress had to have a nail, and if it cost twenty dollars or fifty dollars or whatever for the nails and the extra time to drive them in, then that was what it had to cost. If you cared about the house you were building you drove in enough nails; you didn't rush it and you didn't try to save money that way. Pretty stupid to save a box of nails and lose a perfectly good house because of a bad framing job.

He watched and tried to count. Yes, Johnson was using four to six nails on each stud. But something was wrong. What was it? Suddenly colors swam before him. Red, not blue. Yellow wood with red, not blue at the ends. No. It couldn't be. The lumber had been sitting there since before yesterday; why hadn't he seen it? All spruce studs, yes; but he had ordered blue ends, not red. He took off his hat and strode toward the pile so that he could see the ends of the studs.

Sure enough, there they were: a solid red grill of rectangles stacked one of top of the other, red as blood. And he hadn't even seen them before this. He turned to stare at Johnson, who was nailing away. He paused for only a moment, holding his hat in one hand, rubbing his neck with the other. His forehead and neck felt hot, but sort of dry. He put his hat back on and, walking quickly, made it to the house in an instant, jumping onto the cement floor through a wide space left for a sliding glass door.

"All right, cut it there," he said. Startled, Johnson turned to look at him, holding his hammer in mid-air.

"Just cut it right there," he repeated, walking slowly toward the carpenter. He took the hammer from Johnson's hand. "Don't you know the difference between red and blue studs?" He threw the hammer down. It struck the cement with a painful clang that echoed in the half-enclosed space. It was a horrible thing to treat a tool like that, but he was too angry to care. "You'll have to take all this down. We'll start over with blue ends, just as soon as I can get 'em here. I can't believe you didn't know better than to use the reds."

"Well, sure I knew better," Johnson said shakily. "*I* didn't order 'em. I just figured you knew what you wanted."

"This couldn't have happened with Ben Starritt," Carlyle said. He walked away in disgust, conscious that his head was beginning to ache. He stopped to take his hat off again; behind him Johnson was beginning the hard job of removing nails and tearing out boards. The sweatband of Carlyle's hat was dry, but he felt burning hot. His undershirt stuck some at the small of his back, but it wasn't really wet the way it usually was on a hot day like this. Maybe he shouldn't have stopped at Johnny's and sat in that ice-cold air and then come back out into the humid heat. If he'd been out here all day he'd be sweating the way he should be instead of feeling like a barrowful of dried grass baking under the sun.

His own damn fault anyway for not being here all day, watching out for everything. He should have *noticed* the studs as soon as they were stacked on the lot. No way was he going to settle for red or yellow ends when blue ends were available. Spruce was just spruce to the lumber companies; they charged about the same price for all of it, but any decent carpenter knew blue-ended studs were the strongest, the best. Whether Beaumont would ever know it or not, his house had to be built with blue-ended studs.

As he reached his car he remembered that it was Bob who had been sent to the building supply company. But he was sure that he had given Bob a written order for blue ends. He eased into the car seat; almost worse than the stiffness in his back was the hard pounding of blood at his temples. He wanted to close his eyes, but he had to keep them open in the painful glare on the highway. At the building supply the pain in his head was so bad that he could not vent his wrath on the nervous dispatcher who found the supply slip and admitted the error. The blue studs would be shipped out in the morning.

The next morning he was relieved to see Scovill's small blue truck come bouncing up to the lot.

"First," he said, "we'll have to finish tearing down everything that Johnson did yesterday." He did not ask Scovill about his boy. He just walked briskly up to the house, took a hammer himself and began to remove nails from the yellow boards. "Still can't believe it happened, can't believe that Johnson didn't notice."

"*You* must have seen 'em and *you* didn't notice right off," Scovill said.

"Guess I never much had to, before now," Carlyle said grimly. "Starritt never would have used these."

"Well, that's Starritt. You talk about the guy like he's dead or something, like he was killed in the civil war. Besides, wasn't it *you* ordered the stuff? Or did you send your son after it?"

The nails dropped on to the cement, where they clanged like small, off-key bells.

"Leave my son out of this," Carlyle said. "It was the dispatcher's mistake. Said he'd have the others here this morning." *But we're already two more days behind schedule.*

They worked in silence. Johnson joined them. Then Bob drove up and helped take down the walls that had been roughed-in by Johnson the day before. Bob asked Scovill about Scovill junior; the kid was all right so far as the specialist could tell, but they would just have to wait and see.

When the new lumber arrived, Bob helped the men get it off the truck and then pack up the other load. Scovill and Johnson started the rough-in all over again, beginning with the area Johnson had done the day before. They worked fast. Maybe they were going to try to catch up, to make up for the lost time. Carlyle watched them in the late morning heat, listening to the smooth, firm sound of nails being driven into blue end studs. He watched and listened more carefully. Scovill was quick as a cat, moving as fast as anyone could. Carlyle listened. There was a rhythm to it, but it was a careless rhythm: Scovill picked up one of the long flesh-colored boards and heaved it into upright position, held it there with one hand, took a nail from his mouth with the other, and drove the nail into the board. *One!* Carlyle counted. Then Scovill took another nail from his mouth with his hammer hand and drove it in at the bottom of the board. *Two!* And then Scovill moved on. Carlyle forced himself to watch a while longer before he went up to Scovill, sure of what he had seen, feeling a painful weight in his head, pressing against his eyes.

"What do you think is going to hold up this house, Scovill? Huh? Your lucky guesses?"

Johnson and Scovill stopped working. Scovill turned and glared at him.

"What is it now, Simpson? We took out the old work and we're doing it over. What's your problem?"

"Nails, dammit! You damn smart aleck son of a bitch, it's *nails* hold together a rough-in, and you know it. Maybe on other jobs you're used to skimping so you can save a few bucks, but you aren't going to skimp on nails here! Not on one of *my* houses! Takes twice as many nails as you've been using, and you know it." Carlyle wanted to strike him, but suddenly he stopped. He did not take the hammer from Scovill's hand as he had planned to. The taller man looked down at him, and Carlyle saw a challenge in that look. At that moment he became certain Scovill was deliberately trying to botch the job.

He became conscious that he was working harder than if he were loading cinder blocks on a truck.

"Either you put in four nails per board, or I will," he said.

Scovill's long arm swung in an arc as he indicated the empty house in a careless inclusive shrug.

"Mister, I'm sick of you telling me what to do, as if I don't know what I'm doing. You hired me, dammit, you needed a carpenter and you hired me. Who's the carpenter here? You want me here, you leave me alone. It was supposed to be *my* job to order the studs, in the first place."

So now Scovill was going to pretend that the wrong lumber wouldn't have been delivered if *he'd* done the ordering.

"I'm not gonna let you use two nails and think that's all right. I'm not gonna let you do that to this house," Carlyle said, almost in a whisper. "You're an ass as a carpenter, Scovill." He started to reach for the hammer, but stopped. Scovill held the hammer tightly; his breathing was loud, as it had been on the day of the accident.

"Don't touch it, mister." Scovill backed away, still holding the hammer. "I've had enough of you. Find yourself another carpenter."

Johnson packed up and left right after him.

Carlyle stood and watched them each drive away. Bob hung around, looking at him. He didn't say anything. When Carlyle picked up a couple of two-by-fours and started nailing them himself, Bob began to stack up the lumber Johnson and Scovill had left on the floor. But Carlyle's back hurt too much, he couldn't really do that kind of work. He stopped, and sat down on a pile of lumber. Bob finished and fidgeted.

"You'd better go on home," Carlyle said bitterly. "There's nothing you can do here today."

"Well," Bob said uncertainly. "I hope . . . Well . . ."

Finally, he left too, and Carlyle was left alone, with a house behind schedule, blue-end two-by-fours waiting to be nailed, and no carpenters.

A fire was burning at the edges of all the words that kept curling up from the heat in his brain. All of this because of a few nails and a kid falling off a ladder. Everything had happened so fast, like a fire grabbing hold and leaping to burn things you thought were safe. His words got away from him like that. But there wasn't any way out of it. He couldn't let Scovill go on like that. He would just have to find someone else.

Shortly after he got home, Beaumont called. He wanted to know about the accident. No, Carlyle said, the accident wasn't serious. Scovill's son, wasn't it? Yes, Scovill's son. And by the way, Scovill quit today.

Now a new gust of questions would blow up.

"Quit! Because of the accident?"

No, not because of the accident. Because he and Scovill did not see eye to eye on how a carpenter should do his work. No, he didn't know who he was going to get to replace Scovill. He was sorry, he knew the house was behind schedule, he knew Beaumont wanted to move in before October, and he could only say that he would do his damndest to have the house ready in time.

"Well, let me know what's happening." And then Beaumont surprised him. "Why don't you take a couple days off and then see about a carpenter, Carlyle? You sound like you could use some rest."

He didn't answer that directly, although he wanted to. He felt like saying, just because I'm retired, don't think I can't handle this job, Harold! He was tired. He let it go.

It was already 7:30 by the time he stepped from the early evening heat into the dry cold of Johnny's. He had noticed the sign outside, inviting any and all to arm-wrestle for fun. He did not know who might see the sign and drive in off the highway. They would shake hands and look him in the eye, all the time thinking that they could put his arm down flat on the table. Some would hope to hurt him as they did it. They would think he was presumptuous, a nervy old guy trying to say he was better than they were. Let them think all they wanted, none of them would pin his arm to the table.

The dark brown formica table top looked like wood. It had been moved to the center of the room. As soon as Carlyle sat down, Vicki brought a pitcher of beer and gave him a peck on the cheek.

"Good luck tonight, Carly. I'll be rootin' for you."

Nelson came from the bar and sat down. He flexed his muscles, first one arm, then the other. Without a word he made a fist and faked a punch at Carlyle, reaching halfway across the table. Then he broke into a grin. Carlyle envied, for the hundredth time at least, Nelson's dark hair and good teeth. They weren't perfectly white, but they looked healthy, strong and even.

"Guess you need some warming up," Nelson said, putting his right arm on the table. They locked their fingers together and began to struggle. Carlyle let Nelson have some play, just as he might do with a strong fish he was testing a new rod with: he knew he would land the fish eventually, but he liked to feel the strength of the line resisting the tug of the fish.

After he had enjoyed the play, he brought his arm down and pushed Nelson's tanned, hairy forearm flat against the cool formica. Nelson's eyes held Carlyle's for a moment; Nelson knew better than to appear startled, but he seemed unwilling to let go. Carlyle hated it when anyone, even Nelson, looked into his eyes with intensity, and he was relieved when Nelson finally looked down for a moment. When he looked up again, his gaze was not so sharp, and he was grinning.

"I guess you're warmed up all right," he said.

He did not comment on Carlyle's strength, though they both knew it was surprising, in a man of Carlyle's size. But what pushed the other man's arm to the table was something inside Carlyle, something that grew in his gut and seemed to reach through his arm; he knew what it came from: bitterness. He did not like to think about it.

The money grew in Johnny's bucket. Carlyle wrestled everybody in the room and beat them all. They were mostly regulars, but there were three strangers who had seen the sign. When he had finished with them, the pitcher of beer was empty. He felt warm, flushed from the exertion, but he wasn't sweating.

It was close to nine-thirty when a group of four men came in. They did not look familiar. They were probably in their early twenties, construction workers maybe, with tanned muscular arms. They wore old blue jeans, T-shirts and caps. They were pretty loud; evidently they had already been drinking.

"Where's this wrestling match?" the tallest one bellowed to the room at large.

"Look at this dump!" a second one said; his face was pitted by acne.

Nelson was sitting at the bar. He turned around and got Johnny's bucket.

"You wanna challenge the champion, put your money on here," he said. He did not look at any of them directly.

He explained the rules to them, while they dug out their money.

Carlyle decided he was tired, but not too tired to take them on. He had wrestled all the regulars, they all had known he would win. There had been about ten of them. Then there were the three strangers, about Nelson's age or a little younger. But these guys who had just come in were different; they would not accept a defeat without making trouble. Behind the bar, Johnny was watching them while he dried some glasses. He brushed one palm across the artificial smoothness of the Formica. Not a blemish, not a wrinkle. The empty pitcher in the center of the table left rings, but they would disappear when the table was wiped, even if they were left for days. And the scattered glasses of beer left marks which would disappear the moment Vicki sponged them. That was the great thing about Formica.

The four men came to his table with their pitcher of beer. The table was rectangular and there were eight chairs around it. Johnny wanted plenty of room for spectators. The tall one set the pitcher down hard at the end of the table farthest from Carlyle.

"So you're the man to arm-wrestle here, huh?" he said.

"I guess that's right."

Two of them were still standing. The one with acne rolled up the short sleeves of his T-shirt and flexed his muscles.

"My friend here wants to wrestle you," the tall one said. "Okay?" His thick dark eyebrows nearly met above his nose. He needed a haircut.

Carlyle pointed to the chair opposite his. Acne sat down. Three of them were sitting opposite Carlyle and Eyebrows was at the head of the table. The table had been crowded during the first matches but this time no one came to sit down and watch. Nelson and the others were watching from a distance.

Eyebrows poured beer into four glasses and passed them to his friends. They were not going to offer any to Carlyle. He kept his face expressionless and put up his arm, bringing his elbow down a bit carelessly. He remained impassive despite the sudden pain. As soon as his arm was in position, Acne reached over and seized his hand with an unexpected biting grip. He did not like the man's style, his pocked face, the visor of his cap pulled low over his expressionless grey eyes. His bulging biceps were streaked with dirt. For sure these were construction workers.

They were deadlocked for what seemed a long time. They looked a little surprised. Carlyle was used to that look. Eyebrows took a pack of cigarettes — Scovill's brand — from the rolled-up sleeve of his T-shirt and lit it. Suddenly Carlyle was acutely aware of the stale, poisoned air in the dark bar, the accumulated smoke that hung on for days, along with the sour smell of old beer. He was relieved when Vicki brought over a pint-sized can of Bud and a glass. She opened the can, poured it for him and left it next to his left hand. He did not like to drink while he was wrestling; he had some idea that using his left hand would impair his concentration, maybe take strength from his right arm. But he was thirsty.

"Don't give that man no beer," Eyebrows said to Vicki. "He's already got a beer gut. He don't need no more beer."

"Well, I guess a little more won't hurt him," Vicki said. She laughed. "What's life for anyway, if you can't enjoy it?" Then before she walked away, she asked Eyebrows if she could get him another pitcher of beer for his *friends*.

Vicki was all right. She could tell people off without making them mad. Helen could do it too; he'd seen her stick up for her minister when some of the church people were running him down behind his back.

He raised his left hand and drank the fresh beer. It washed away the smoky sour air that had caught in his throat. Eyebrows blew smoke through his nose and pulled his cap lower over his forehead. Acne was weakening. Sweat was dripping from his face; he shifted his body, using his shoulders and back to get leverage. Carlyle wondered why he wasn't sweating more himself.

Acne was weakening. Carlyle gathered up all the fierce, sour hatred he felt for these men and pushed suddenly hard. He had not intended to hurt him, but the man grunted in pain. Carlyle held his arm to the table a moment longer than he had to, before he released him, and finished off his beer. Acne moved his arm slowly; he could not resist rubbing it.

One of his friends said, "Whatsa matter, Bill? Old man too much for you, huh?"

Eyebrows did not join in the ribbing. He was staring at Carlyle.

Vicki brought Carlyle another beer. He hoped the others would not order another pitcher. Acne stood up to leave and the two others rose, but they stood and waited while Eyebrows sat in his chair glowering at Carlyle.

"I'm going to have to wrestle you to get my money back," he said. "I guess my friends here didn't know old men can be ornery. But I can teach an old man a thing or two about Injun wrestling."

One of them went to speak to Nelson about the envelopes in the bucket. Carlyle was tired. But he put his arm up and accepted Eyebrows' fierce bony grip. The other men remained standing this time, to watch. Carlyle grunted despite himself as his arm was pushed toward the table. This man had a strength that he had not suspected; he was slighter than his friend Bill, even though he was taller. Carlyle's elbow burned, grinding into the dark Formica. The beer had not removed the dry sour taste in his mouth. His arm was being pushed farther toward the table; it was a third of the way now. His veins swelled. He gripped Eyebrows' hand with all his might; he would not let go, he would not lose hold.

He stared into his opponent's eyes because he did not want to look up and see astonishment on Johnny's face, or Nelson's. He saw two small, dull green eyes, like cloudy marbles. Beneath them was a long nose and thin lips, which were the only horizontal lines in that elongated face. The long, powerful right arm slowly forced Carlyle's arm flat onto the table top, which was sticky with beer. And he held it there, just as Carlyle had done to his friend. The pain was excruciating. Carlyle thought suddenly of Duffy and the fifty dollars Duffy had been ready to bet on a loser.

Afterward there was a lot of joking. Everybody tried to make light of the whole thing. The four men had won back their money and most of the rest of the money in the bucket. Eyebrows was the first one out of the place, but one of the four who had only watched, stayed for a moment near the table and said loudly to the room, "Well, he did all right for an old man . . ." It was probably meant to be a compliment.

Old man, old man. Probably Scovill and everyone else who worked for him called him that, even though he was always showing them that he could do what old men could not. But then there were the things he couldn't do any more. He couldn't drive without pain in his back, he couldn't heave cement bags or two-by-fours the way he used to. He was used to all kinds of aches and pains. But that didn't make a man old, not if the man kept on his feet and didn't give way to it like Helen, sitting around and getting stiff and fat.

He sat back, drank more beer and reminded himself to smile because his friends were trying to cheer him up.

"Hey, Carly, that guy must be a pro. His friend said he's never been beat."

"I think he's part Polish or nigger, one or the other."

"Shit, he's an imported mongrel from Russia. Did you see the eyebrows on him?"

"Mongol, stupid!" Nelson shouted. "Right, Carly?"

"Right." They knew he wasn't in the mood for joking. He finished his beer and got up. He said he was sorry about the money they had lost on him; he had enjoyed it anyway, but he had to go home now. He knew better than to offer to pay back the money. He promised himself he would make a big contribution to Johnny's bucket when the next bet came up. Nelson slapped him on the back; automatically he shrugged away.

"Hey," Nelson said.

He walked slowly into the humid air. His back was stiff and his arm really hurt. He took his time unlocking his Ford and easing into the front seat. He rolled down the window and sat for a few minutes, listening to the rush of cars on the highway. Everybody going somewhere, wherever people went at night. Out to drink, to forget about things, or they went home, to watch themselves and their families getting older, to fight about money. Maybe some of them had a place they wanted to go to, someone they wanted to be with.

That was all over for him, but he was not going to go around crying over it. Maybe that was what it was to grow old: you didn't have any place you wanted to go, or anybody you really wanted to be with any more. Those things were for young men for a while, cocky men who didn't even know they had them until after they lost them — the places and the people they had.

He thought of going back inside again. He really wanted a couple of shots of bourbon. But if he went back inside now, they would see — what? He wasn't sure, but he wouldn't go back in. He opened his mouth and drew in air that felt cool to his throat but left no moisture inside him. He supposed it was Duffy he wanted and some fishing on a foggy morning. He might be too tired and stiff even to fish.

He looked down at his stomach, rolling over the top of his Bermuda shorts, covered by his sport shirt, but certainly not hidden. *He* should talk about Helen! He wasn't as fat as she was, but he sure had his own beer gut; Maybe those bastards were right. He was a rundown old asshole; they thought he had never done a damn thing in his life but sit around and arm-wrestle and drink beer. That was probably all he was good for now, except maybe the arm-wrestling would go next. He wondered what would have happened if he had taken the hammer from Mr. Rodney Scovill. Scovill could have killed him, he was sure of that. Or he might have killed Scovill. Bashed in the brain in that head that was nearly six inches higher than his own. Bash it in and then build Beaumont's house. It didn't take a tall man to build a house; a house was something you had to see in your mind to keep alive until you finished putting it up. You built it in the bright sunlight and you didn't build it to hide things in either. But some people, like Helen, would never understand that.

He started the car and backed out. Pulling onto the highway, he noticed Johnny's sign in the rear-view mirror: "Come Arm-Wrestle the Champ! Tonight at 8." Somewhere in this town he was going to find another carpenter, someone not much worse than Scovill. Not a Carlyle Simpson carpenter, but someone who would do.

SEVEN

BURNING

In the morning he found a large breakfast of ham and eggs waiting for him, still hot. For once Helen had timed it right. The pink ham glistened, with tiny beads of juice. Helen sat drinking her hot tea and dipping her toast in it as usual.

Between bites, he said, "The ham's good. Not too dry this time."

"It's the same ham cooked the same way as I always cook it... But there won't be any ham or any other meat tomorrow if you don't give me some money for groceries. You were supposed to give it to me last week."

"Oh, sure, more money," he snapped back. "What the hell, you think I got plenty of it." He thought of Duffy's fifty dollars and of all the bets lost on the match, including his own fifty. He shook his head, dug out his wallet and handed her a twenty. "You'll get the rest later." He watched her crumple the twenty and put it in her housecoat pocket. Her face looked determined, her lips pursed tight. "Always going to the store to buy something," he muttered, half to her, half to himself. he finished his breakfast without much pleasure. She did not say — as she had on rare occasions worked up the nerve to say — that he was no one to talk, the way he spent more at bars every day than she spent on groceries in a week. Instead, she finished her tea and toast and carried her cup and saucer to the kitchen. When she came back to clear away his dishes, he said, "I'm not going to the site today. Got some other things to take care of."

She stayed out of his way. He went into his office and phoned three carpenters he had heard other contractors say good things about. He called them even though he considered the recommendations next to worthless, because it came from men whose work he did not really respect. They all three said no, they weren't available — two wives spoke for husbands who were at work. He decided he might as well mow the lawn, although it was a little earlier in the day than he liked. The grass would be drier at noon, but he was glad to go to the garage and busy himself getting the mower out and checking its fuel level. The engine started loud and strong.

The grass smelled sweet in the humid morning air. He cut in long, even swathes; he couldn't hear anything through the steady, sure noise of the mower's engine. There were no surprises, no questions or arguments. No one would bother him here. He relaxed, taking his time. There was no need to hurry today. He couldn't do anything at the site.

Beaumont going ahead and telling him to take a couple days off. What was that really supposed to mean? That he was too old, maybe, too old to handle supplies and workers and deadlines? Well, maybe Beaumont was right; maybe he should take a day or two off and go fishing. But the boat was in being repaired.

When he finished mowing the front, he carted the wheelbarrowful of grass he had collected down to his vacant lot at the end of the street. The pavement felt hot through his shoes and socks. The pile of old grass was still in the lot; he would have to burn some of it later today. As he came back up the street he saw with satisfaction the neat even rows of his mowing. The grass looked hot, as though the green blades had drawn heat up through the soil and held it. The soil under the grass would be cool, of course, while the thick green blades baked in the sun. The heat was lying everywhere today like a weight; it sat on the lawn and on the pavement. As he climbed back onto the mower he took off his hat and touched his barely damp forehead with his fingers, wondering why he wasn't sweating any more.

After he finished the back lawn he went inside. Helen asked him what he would like for lunch. He could not think of anything. Helen's faded housedress was printed with what had once been bright red and yellow flowers, unusually cheerful even for Helen's taste. The faded colors made her look even paler. Her skin was colorless, as though there were no blood pulsing beneath it. He thought suddenly of Eyebrows' tan arms and shook his head. No. He would not think about that man, or about Scovill, or about any of the men at the site and at Johnny's. Bob had walked away.

He told Helen he did not want lunch; he was going to lie down for a while and maybe after that he would eat something. He was hot and tired and his back ached from lifting the bags full of grass into the wheelbarrow. Probably Bob was thinking the old man got what he deserved, yelling at Johnson and Scovill. Well, who the hell cared. They were always accusing him of something — Bob or Helen or Sarah, or the men who worked for him. Gutless wonders. He was glad to be alone in his bedroom where he didn't have to talk to anybody.

That afternoon he burned the dried grass that had been sitting piled up on the vacant lot for weeks. Mrs. Martin's car was in the driveway, but he did not care whether she was home or not. He was a busy man and had to burn when he could. When he had the fire burning steadily, he went back to the garage and took down his three favorite fishing rods. He could keep an eye on the fire and check his rods and tackle box at the same time.

The green tackle box was cool in his hands. He rubbed away the dust and opened the rusty latch. The contents of the box were more of a mess than he had expected. He couldn't remember when he had last cleaned out the box and gone through the assortment of lures and hooks and sinkers. Long before Duffy died, probably. Slowly he began to pick through the tangled bits of fishing line, to separate the different weights of lead sinkers. He put all the lures he was going to throw out and replace in one pile on the workbench.

He had not been in the garage for long when Helen came in to tell him Mrs. Martin was on the phone, complaining about the smoke.

"I tried to get her calmed down, Carlyle, but she *insisted* that you come to the phone. She said she saw you come back up here, and she didn't want to talk to me."

"So what'd you tell her?"

"I told her I'd see if you would come to the phone."

Helen stood with her hands on her hips, her faded housedress loose about her body; the spindly, hairless legs sticking out beneath it could have been attached to anyone, male or female. If she took off her glasses and he came close to her, she would see him only as a kind of blob, a vague shape of uncertain color — his tan shorts indistinguishable from his white undershirt. Again, he was thankful that his vision, at least, was clear.

"Tell her I got nothing to say to her. Tell her to go out somewhere. I don't care what you tell her!" He turned back to his tackle box and added, not bothering to see whether she still stood there, "Telephones make people think they can bother you anytime they please, right in your own home. We oughta have that damn thing taken out." The telephone and the newspapers. Helen enjoyed them more than he did. Before he retired, the phone had been necessary, but since then he hardly used it. After he finished the Beaumont house he would not need to use it at all, and that would please him as much as never having to look at a Scovill again.

Later, he grew thirsty, and wanted a beer; he did not want to go to Johnny's or any other bar. He couldn't remember if there were any beers in the refrigerator. He knew that if there were any, they wouldn't be cold enough, but he shrugged, left the workbench and went inside.

Every time he opened the refrigerator he wished he hadn't. It was filled with old pots, plates, plastic bowls, covered with tinfoil or left uncovered, neglected, forgotten. At the back of the second shelf, behind a hunk of mashed potatoes uncovered in a cracked, blistered plastic dish, he found a can of beer with a single biscuit, halfway wrapped in foil, on top of it. The biscuit was hard as concrete. Helen was always running from the dinner table to take fresh hot rolls or biscuits from the oven while rolls were already on the table. "Here, have a hot one," she'd say, and then the rolls on the first plate would be wasted. *Waste.* He knocked the hard biscuit into the mashed potatoes and took out the can of beer.

He poured the beer into a glass and took it with him into the living room, where Helen was sitting on the floor with the vacuum cleaner, apparently taking it apart.

"Yeah," he said, after a long drink of beer, "gonna have to have that telephone taken out after this house is finished. We don't need it any more, and I don't like having that old fool calling us all the time."

To his surprise she didn't come back at him, asking why she couldn't at least have a telephone in this house where she didn't have anything else—no decent clothes, no working appliances because he never saw fit to repair or replace anything—that was what she always said when she broke something. Now it looked like she had broken the vacuum cleaner and he'd be damned if he would pay for a new one. And he wasn't going to pay any repair bills because he was damned sick and tired of her carelessness. When they built this house, he had given in and bought her a good dishwasher, and before she had had it two years, she had managed to break it. It sat there, unused, for five years until Bob and Sarah went behind his back and paid a repairman to come in and fix it while he was out. There was a dent in it where he had kicked it the night he had found them using it again. That was the night Sarah had cursed him and run out of the house, saying she would never come back again.

He grinned sourly and quickly drank some beer. That was a long time ago and Sarah had been back many times on visits. The visits hadn't really cancelled out that night. But he hardly ever thought about it.

Helen was still fiddling with the vacuum cleaner. Maybe she was just changing the bag after all. While she was busily putting the cleaner together again, she started to talk without looking at him.

"You know you can't just *ignore* people, Carlyle. Mrs. Martin hung up on me when I told her you couldn't come to the phone. She's really insulted. She knows you just didn't want to talk to her." She stood up and looked at him warily, as though she was ready to leave the room at any moment. "She's going to call the police if you don't stop. You know that. She already said it last time."

He took a step forward and stood near one of the chairs she had insisted on bringing down from Carolina, even though it stuck out in the room like a sore thumb. Helen moved nervously back. "She's going to do it this time, Carlyle, I just know it. Can't you just go and put that fire out now? Before it's too late?"

He burst out into a rage. "Hell no! It's my property and I'll burn on it or do whatever I damn well please on it! Let her call! What are they going to do—arrest me? Let 'em come. They can shoot me before they ever take *me* in!" He gave the chair a kick, sending it over on its back, its legs in the air like some stupid dog playing dead, and stormed out of the room, even more enraged by the shooting pains in his back.

In the garage he threw himself into his seat at the workbench and tried to finish weeding out the tackle box. But he couldn't seem to sit still. Every few minutes he walked out the front of the garage and looked down the street toward the vacant lot and the pile of burning grass. The old cow was downright ornery. What was wrong with the smell of smoke from burning grass? It was a strong smell, but it was a nice one, it came from cleaning, working, taking care of property. Helen should have told the old bitch that there were worse smells in her own house. There were lots of worse smells in the air in summer.

Helen's car started up while he was at the workbench. She was probably going to the grocery store to spend that twenty dollars. Buy more food to waste and ruin. He had often wondered, what would a poor creature like Helen *do* alone? She couldn't survive without someone trying to drum some common sense into her now and then. If it wasn't for the children she probably wouldn't even do the few things she had done; he had to admit she had taken care of them. Even though she was overprotective. She spoiled them, so that they were more her children than his, but he couldn't worry about that any more. You couldn't count on kids respecting their parents no matter what you did. It was always a mystery the way kids turned out. Look at Billy Sanders. Or maybe there was no mystery about his behavior. Pete and Mavis had been too damned good to him, they spoiled him rotten. Naturally he turned out to be a problem.

He put aside the tackle box and picked up one of the rods to test-cast it in the garage. The reel needed adjusting. He could go fishing tomorrow, even without Duffy's boat. Just get on one of those commercial deep-sea jobs. Take the reel with the stronger cast line.

A car door slammed, there was a pause and another slam. Helen had come back and was unloading her groceries. She usually carried them through the garage, but this time she must have decided to use the front door. She was probably hysterical by now. She would watch the clock and look out the windows for police cars, biting her nails the whole time. Probably she would even call Bob and ask him what to do. And if Bob wasn't home she would just wait at the window, helpless and frightened, expecting a police car to come and disgrace her in front of the entire neighborhood. After all, what *would* her church people say?

He smiled, tying a fresh hook, line and sinker. It was nothing but a bluff. And so what if she did call the police? Let 'em come. Hell, he was improving the neighborhood; his lawn upgraded the whole street, and to keep a lawn like that you had to dispose of dead grass. You'd think the old fart would thank him. But that was how they all were. You did something decent, and nobody thanked you for it. They had to get in the way instead, creeping in like snaky St. Augustine into Argentine Bahaia.

He went to the lot to check on the fire. It had gone out. No—he looked more closely, stirring the ashes and the heap of unburned grass. They were *wet*. Somebody had poured water on the fire and stirred it into the heap. On purpose. On *his* lot. He turned and looked at Mrs. Martin's house, trying to see which window she was watching him from. He shook his fist. The old hag had *trespassed* on his property. She had taken matters into her own hands and deliberately sabotaged him. All of the windows in her house were darkened by screens: you couldn't see inside. He shook his fist again, and it occurred to him that she might even be *laughing* at him.

He didn't think the old bitch had the guts. Well, she wasn't going to keep him from burning. He raked up a new pile, carefully separating as much dry grass as he could and moving it farther back on the lot. It took a long time to get the blaze going, but finally it caught like Moses' bush, and then he had to trim it back and watch it. Good. He inhaled the hot, sweet smoke, wishing he had a good country ham from North Carolina and a shed to cure it in.

Later, he left the blaze, hefting the rake like a proud farmer, and went back to the garage, where he watched the street to see if the old fool would sneak out again. This time she would get caught.

The shiny white cruisers came down the street like two white sharks following a current. Casting his heavy test line in the driveway, Carlyle found himself hoping that these sharks were not hungry today. Sure enough, they slowed down as they passed the fire, then came on to his house and parked behind Helen's car in the street. Two policemen got out. They saw him and came walking toward him. The other two stayed put. Why two cruisers? You'd think the police would have better things to do than come running every time some old bitch squawked about something.

He went inside the garage and propped the fishing rod against the wall. The tackle box was now neatly organized, and the tangled fishing line was lying like a mass of thickened spider webs on the bench. He waited angrily for these men who could walk into his life whenever they pleased, just because they wore a uniform.

"Mr. Carlyle Simpson?"

The officer was young and short-haired. He and his older partner stopped just beneath the suspended garage door.

Carlyle nodded. "Yeah, that's me. What can I do for you?"

"Well, we've had a call on you for burning, Mr. Simpson. Violation of city ordinance 83. Complaints that you are endangering the health of your neighbors at that vacant lot down there."

"Yes, it's my lot. Now what law says I can't burn my own grass on my own lot when I want? I've been burning on that lot for years and doing a favor to the neighborhood, if you ask me. Nobody got all hot and bothered about it until Mrs. Martin decided all of a sudden it was ruining her poor little nostrils. I can tell you one thing," and he winked at the officers, "I never had any trouble with that old lady while her husband was alive." They didn't smile. He half wished he were not wearing his dirty white undershirt and his work shorts; these guys were as stiff as two-by-fours.

The door from the house opened, and Helen appeared, looking as though someone had called her. But no one had, he felt like telling her.

"What seems to be the problem?" she asked, in her best polite southern lady voice.

"Well, ma'am," said the young policeman, "we're just here to ask your husband if he won't put out that fire he's burning. Some of the neighbors don't like the smoke."

Carlyle seethed. He did not look at Helen, who kept her distance.

"So I don't like a lot of things about the old crow who called you. I didn't send the police after her," he told them.

The policemen exchanged glances, and then the younger one talked to him as if he were a difficult child. "Mr. Simpson, from what I understand this isn't the first time you've burned grass in that lot. You just acknowledged that yourself. From what I understand, the neighbors have been pretty patient about it."

Carlyle left the tackle box on the bench and stood up, still holding a green lure in his right hand. He wanted to take the lure, the line and the hook and rip it across the young policeman's crisply starched shirt. Riding around in his air-conditioned cruiser all day, feeling important intruding on people's property. Why wasn't he out tracking down drug dealers instead of chasing after good citizens? Young wise punks get a uniform and that's all they need to make them behave like real assholes.

Sounds of static and fragments of the dispatcher's voice came from the radios in the two cruisers.

"You're creating a public nuisance, Mr. Simpson. Now either you put out the fire or we'll put it out and arrest you for creating a disturbance."

Carlyle glared, gripping the lure tightly.

"Arrest me? Look, young fella, why don't you go arrest *her,* for God's sake — she's already trespassed on *my* property!"

"Now, Carlyle," Helen began, as though she could hear the anger rising in his voice, as if she thought he was going to make a fool of himself.

"Shut up, woman! You don't know anything! You go get that damned old bitch Martin on the damned telephone yourself and *ask* her. Ask her who in the hell did she think I'd think it was, trespassing on my lot and pouring water on my fire?" He turned to the policemen, gripping the lure in his fist. "You go ahead and arrest me, officers, but you'll have to arrest that old idiot down the street too. You go down and see for yourself she put out the fire I had going. You think I'm a nuisance? I'll tell you who's a nuisance. That old hag's always meddling, never leaves me alone — and how about that goddam minister next door, did you see that lawn of his? *That's* a public nuisance! You're damned right there's a disturbance in this neighborhood when an old senile fool can have the only man arrested who keeps a decent lawn and tries to do anything right around here!"

The policeman's voice was soothing. "Okay, I see. But what do you say we go down and talk with Mrs. Martin, Mr. Simpson, and maybe you two can clear this thing up together, huh? If she really did trespass, it wouldn't solve anything to arrest her —"

"The hell it wouldn't! What do you mean, if she really did trespass? I saw the ashes. She's the only one who could —"

"She's not," Helen said in a high voice. "Please calm down —"

He hated the pleading in her voice.

"NO!" He didn't care who heard his raised voice. "No! She's a sneaky old hag and she's not going to get away with it. She's damn well gonna have to tell me to my face that she didn't trespass on my property!"

Helen's face wrinkled like a frightened rabbit's nose. The older policeman said, "Now look. Let's just calm down."

"She didn't," Helen said, in her frightened, nervous voice. "She didn't, Carlyle. *I* did it. I snuck out and poured water on the fire."

He stared at her with his mouth open; his legs felt numb and suddenly tired. He loosened his grip on the lure and noticed for the first time that the hook had caught him; his palm and fingers were bloody. He looked at her hunched shoulders. She hung there like a wrinkled towel.

Quietly he said, "I'll get my rake, one second."

He took the rake with him and went to fill and empty the fertilizer bucket with water at the outside spigot. The two policemen went with him to the lot and stood there while he poured water on the fire and stirred the ashes and poured again and raked again. They didn't seem to know what to say when he asked them what he was supposed to do, why a man couldn't even burn his own dead grass on his own vacant lot, to keep his own lawn healthy.

Later he found her in the kitchen, chopping onions for her chicken casserole. The veins stood out on the backs of her hands like pale lavender yarn. It always surprised him to notice how bony her fingers were, a couple of knuckles jutted out like minor deformities.

There was an open can of cream of mushroom soup on the counter, and the frozen chicken lay thawing in the sink. The sight of the milky beige blob of condensed soup disgusted him. He watched her arrange the ingredients in the casserole dish, dumping the thick glob of soup on the chicken like so much rotten gravy you wouldn't feed to a dog. He shook his head and opened his mouth to tell her that with the money she spent on groceries, there was no excuse to feed him slop, and what business was it of hers to go around putting out fires. But before he could speak, the kitchen wall phone began to ring and she went to answer it. He went into the dining room, slowly pulled out his chair and sat down.

"Yes, of course they came, Eleanor. I know perfectly well you saw them." Helen sounded irritated. There were a series of tinny squeaks. When he was in the dining room and Helen was in the kitchen on the telephone he could often hear these voices on the other end of the line, sounding like distant stations on the radio.

Mrs. Martin went on squeaking for a long time. The bird feeders in the back yard looked low; he would have to fill them.

"Now wait a minute, Eleanor. That's not true. He has *not* been deliberately provoking you. He has to burn — that's the only way he can get rid of the dead grass. He doesn't want his lot to look like an eyesore. You *know* he's not a spiteful man." It was the way she had talked to the children when they were upset about some supposed injustice at school. "You know how husbands are, Eleanor," Helen said. "You can tell them and tell them but they don't take anything seriously unless someone tells them who isn't their wife." Poor Helen. Pretending he was just like other women's husbands. It made him feel small and mean to hear her. But then he thought of that mush in the glass dish with the chicken, and his stomach constricted.

All that goose grease must have worked. "Oh sure," Helen said, "you're right. We've got to get together sometime soon and have a real nice chat. He just had no idea how upset you were. You know, they never listen."

He went back out to the garage. There was a cool breeze blowing in from the bay and it was nice and quiet. He finished clearing off the workbench; his hand felt pretty sore. In the half-bath between the garage and the kitchen he scrubbed the caked blood away and poured merthiolate into the cuts.

It was fishing he wanted, he decided the next morning, as he stood fully dressed in the driveway. He felt alert and clear-headed despite the drinks he had had the night before. It was still dark; he had snapped awake suddenly, and hadn't been able to go back to sleep. Helen was not up yet, thank God.

He could not see beyond the driveway. Around the street lamp there was a fine, heavy mist; the white globe a blob of soft light which could not penetrate the black more than a few feet. But this early the air, though humid as usual, was still cool and refreshing.

He decided to call Bob, and went back inside to the kitchen. He turned on the light and saw two large palmetto bugs helping themselves to crumbs on the floor near the stove. If you pulled out the refrigerators in many Florida houses, you would find the bodies of several large bugs. The warmth drew them like flies to manure. Seeing a few roaches always made him wonder about all the others he didn't see. You built a nice house like this and the roaches took it over because Helen didn't keep it clean. It was disgusting.

He rummaged in one of Helen's crammed drawers for the phone book; Bob's number was written on the inside cover.

When Bob realized who was calling he seemed to wake up. No, Carlyle couldn't remember having called him before, either. Yes, he guessed it must be something of a surprise.

"You want me at the site today?" Bob asked, cautiously. "Did you get the frame and trim done, or what?"

Carlyle stiffened. "No, I didn't get it done. You know Scovill quit on me." *Don't act like you weren't there, either.*

"Gosh, you mean you still haven't found anybody?"

"No, I haven't got anybody yet. Listen, that's not what I'm calling about. I want to catch one of those commercial deep-sea charters. You want to come along, or what?"

"Today? Right now?"

"Yes, I mean today. Now."

Bob put his hand over the phone; he heard muffled voices. So the kid was sleeping with his girlfriend. Well, that shouldn't surprise him. Nowadays all the guys could get it free; it wasn't like before. And Bob probably gave the girl dope and who knows what else. It wasn't pleasant to think of your son as a bum who would get what he could out of girls, but Bob wasn't the kind to mistreat anyone. But why couldn't the kid straighten up and make something of himself? Why couldn't he just stay with construction, if he really liked it, and go somewhere with it?

"Listen, if you've got other plans," he began, but the phone was still muffled. After a minute Bob's voice came through again.

"Okay, sure, Pop. You want me to meet you at the marina? Which one do you have in mind?"

"You're sure you can do this? You don't have other plans?"

"No, no—that sounds great. Tell me where."

So he told Bob where to meet him and hung up and turned off the light, leaving the roaches to enjoy the few remaining minutes of darkness, and went to get his fishing gear.

They met at the marina just in time to catch the 6:30 commercial deep sea charter. Neither spoke for the first fifteen or twenty minutes; they drank hot coffee from white styrofoam cups and watched the whitecaps in the wake.

The Gulf, an inscrutable surface, was a dull green this morning; the sun was not yet high enough to reflect off it.

Soon after the captain anchored the boat, Carlyle cast his line and refrained from commenting when it took Bob three attempts to cast decently.

"I haven't been out fishing since the last time we went," Bob said.

"You kept the rod, I see." The rod he had given Bob for Christmas, what was it—his twelfth birthday? Something like that.

"Well, sure I kept it. I wouldn't think of getting rid of it." *Just like his mother, never gets rid of anything.*

He felt a tug and pulled. A ripple broke the calm surface: he reeled in a medium-sized grouper, deftly removed the hook and laid it in the bucket. He baited the line again and recast, inhaling deeply. He liked the feel of the damp salt air on his dry skin; he wished it could draw out the moisture from his body, and make him sweat the way he used to.

He pulled in another as Bob watched and was relieved when Bob reeled in his own large grouper.

"Good catch," he said.

Bob smiled and relaxed in his chair; his bony spine curved out a pocket in the green nylon webbing.

"So," he said, "you got anybody in mind for a carpenter yet?"

"Nope. Got to keep looking."

He felt another tug; he could see it was small. He reeled it in and threw it back, rebaited and recast.

"Well," he said, "at least they're biting today."

"Yeah, they sure are. Say, listen Pop, I might know somebody. He just works as a carpenter in the summers, but I think he's pretty good."

"Yeah?"

"Yeah. I don't know if you . . . and I'm not even sure he's available. But I know he's in town and I know he's done quite a bit of carpentry summers up north."

"Why just summers?"

"Well, he was in school . . . He's a friend of Sarah's from college."

"Oh, so I guess Sarah asked you to help him out."

"*No*, Pop. She doesn't even know I . . . And maybe he's busy. I just thought . . . But listen, if you don't like the idea, forget it."

Well, after all he needed a carpenter. How good would some kid Sarah's age be? Well, maybe no worse than Scovill.

"You heard from Sarah lately?" He tried to say it casually.

"Couple of weeks ago." Bob concentrated on his rod. The old secrecy. Bob would never talk about Sarah with him. Always did cover up for her, played big brother. Probably fed her resentment, told her every little thing the old man did.

"So how's she doing?"

"She's doing fine. Probably coming down next week. Say, weren't you going to stop in and see her while you were in Carolina?"

"That was your mother's idea. I couldn't make it."

They both watched the gulf, waiting. Neither had a bite.

"Say," Bob said, "how are they all in Carolina? How was your trip? How's everybody?"

"They're all right," Carlyle said. "Pete was having some trouble with Billy. Weird kid. Spent most of my time helping Pete try to chase him down. Ran away. He didn't get far. If you ask me he's not *right*. If you know what I mean."

"No, Pop. I don't know what you mean."

He hated that superior, deliberate tone of theirs.

"He was having some trouble," he said calmly. "The kid's afraid he's one of those. You know." He hated to say it, it was too disgusting. "Queer. He thinks he's queer."

Bob kept his eyes on the water. The sun was reflecting now with an almost painful glare.

"Spoiled him too much, that's what did it," Carlyle said. "He's never had to face anything like a man."

Bob stood up. "I think I'll go below for a minute."

"Hey now, I was just making a simple observation. Queers are queers, you know, that's a fact. Guys with earrings . . ." His laughter sounded tinny in his own ears. "At least I know my son ain't like that. Sounded like you had a nice something in your bed this morning." He reached over to slap Bob's thigh, but the boy sprang back quicker than an arching cat. He was already gone, his rod lying on the deck.

Carlyle was surprised to notice that he wasn't angry. Like Helen. The poor kid had no sense of humor. Couldn't take a joke. Always hot and bothered about other people's rights. Just like Helen. Over sensitive.

He sat relaxed, listening to the quiet lapping of the water against the boat, the murmur of conversation from other fishermen farther down the deck.

Bob came back and picked up his rod in silence. Carlyle had added three fish to the bucket and before the captain turned the boat around they had each added two more. Grouper and one red snapper that Carlyle could be proud of. They would be back by one o'clock; it hadn't been a bad morning. Bob went and got a soda for himself and a Bud for Carlyle. Peace offering.

"Pretty good catch," Carlyle said.

"Yeah."

"How about a sandwich?" He bought dry, tasteless roast beef sandwiches for both of them. But they weren't too bad with the beer. The water glared in the sunlight; even with his straw hat on, Carlyle could not bear to look at it. He kept his eyes on the deck and on his scuffed white summer shoes.

"Well, so who's this carpenter fellow? You got a number?"

"Well, yeah, I've got his number. But listen, Pop . . . I hope . . . I hope you'll be careful . . ."

Carlyle tensed: he felt his neck jerk.

"How do you mean?"

"Oh, don't get mad. I know you want everything just so, I mean . . . But there are ways to tell people . . . They're not your slaves . . ."

Carlyle could see apprehension in the nervous glances Bob was throwing at him. He wished he could push down his anger, but there it was, solid, like the cinder block. It was weighing him down in the flimsy aluminum chair. He gripped the arms hard to keep from standing and raising his fist. He waited to answer until his breath came more freely.

"All right," he said in a low hard voice. "You make up your goddamn mind. You want me to try him or not? The guy can always say no if he wants to, can't he? Or is he a goddamn queer too?"

Bob swallowed his sandwich with an effort.

"Okay," he said. "You call him. What the hell. And there's something else you ought to know. Sarah's coming down next week because Mom's going into the hospital. I guess she was afraid to tell you. She's got to go into the hospital so they can find out what's wrong with her. She's been feeling bad for a long time."

The boat slowed and pulled into its deck slip. The captain's son, a slow hefty boy, threw the fat ropes securely around the wooden posts. They caught and the boat steadied into a slow rocking.

EIGHT

NOISES
AND ECHOES

Mortimer Pascagouli was a big tall hunk of a man. He walked around the site bare-chested, sweating heavily, with a dirty white terry cloth sweatband across his forehead; his shock of thick hair splashed over it like a wet black mop. He mumbled a lot; he told Carlyle he was reciting Italian poetry. Pascagouli was a drop-out from graduate school.

"I just threw it up, Mr. Simpson. I asked myself what I was doing there, the old Being and Essence question and I couldn't approach the why. So I gave it up and took up my present employment."

Mortimer never interrupted his work while he talked. The sweat rolled off his meaty shoulders, down his spine into his baggy pants and his whole torso glistened. He seemed to soak up the sun, to collect heat like a solar converter and send it back out again in liquid form.

He worked fast and his hands reminded Carlyle of Ben Starritt's; he knew a line of wood and how to fit it together properly. "Of course, nothing is ever plumb, level or square, Mr. Simpson," Pascagouli said, "that is only a supposition like all other suppositions. But don't take me literally, I'm not speaking literally."

Carlyle gave up early trying to understand Mortimer Pascagouli. He stopped answering and just nodded a lot. He went on with his work, checking his schedule or his order sheets, sweeping out the house and occasionally nailing a few of the remaining two-by-fours.

"Ought to be a damn lawyer," he said to Nelson when, at the end of the week he set foot in Johnny's for the first time since the arm-wrestling fiasco. "The way he talks. But he can talk and work at the same time. I haven't seen a carpenter with hands like that since old Ben Starritt."

"Watch who you're callin' old, mister!" Nelson said.

"Yeah, well, all I got to say is, that's one eye-talian I gotta hand it to: he's a damned sight better than Scovill and I was damned lucky to get him."

Some days Pascagouli wore glasses, big glasses in ugly black plastic frames that made him look goofy. Other days he'd come to work without them, or leave them in a case which kept dropping out of his hip pocket. Didn't he need them to see? Evidently not; he was fitting wood together by intuition, maybe, by touch. And he threw away wood. Carlyle liked that. Out of a hundred blue-end studs, Pascagouli would throw away fifteen or more. He crowned the studs in the wall so that all the humps in the wood went one way. He held the studs carefully, feeling their weight and balance. Carlyle, watching, could tell.

Bob mentioned that he had run into Scovill's kid; he seemed fine, except that he moved kind of funny. But he had always done that, Bob said. Carlyle just grunted. He wanted to forget Mr. Rodney Scovill.

By the end of the week Pascagouli had finished building out the interior walls and together they had nailed the furring strips into the concrete block walls every sixteen feet. Pascagouli didn't really need to be shown how to do things. When Beaumont stopped at the site on Friday afternoon, Carlyle was able to tell him that they were nearly back on schedule. The buck strips for the windows were in and just that day Carlyle and Pascagouli had hung the windows together.

It was a good thing that Pascagouli was as big as he was, because the windows were heavy gauge anodized aluminum, mostly single-hung; nine of these with only three awning windows at the back of the house, on either side of the sliding glass doors. Single-hung windows, along with the raised roof, gave the house more of the "colonial" effect that Beaumont wanted, to keep it from looking like all the other concrete block Florida houses with their flat roofs. Anodized aluminum pushed up the total cost of materials by nearly a hundred and twenty dollars, but Carlyle would not use mill windows, extruded aluminum, as most other contractors did. He and Beaumont went down the list together.

"You might just as well put in the decent windows first thing, Harold, or you'll be sorry later," Carlyle said. "If that aluminum isn't anodized you know what the salt and the humidity are going to do to it in ten years."

Beaumont stood a foot taller than Carlyle. He had a healthy

ruddy complexion. "Yeah, I guess you're right, Carly. Now that you
mention it, I *have* seen that stuff corrode."

"I've got anodized windows in my own house," Carlyle said,
"and they're just as shiny now as the day they were put in."

"Okay." Beaumont went cursorily down the list again, checking
the figures. "Everything seems great. Of course I don't like the way
prices have gone up, but there isn't much we can do about that, is
there?"

Carlyle spat on the sandy dirt in what would soon be Beaumont's
front yard. His nose and mouth felt rough and dry; his mouth held
its sour taste. He took the check Beaumont handed him — the first
payment — folded it and shook his head. "Don't know what anybody
can do about it."

"You think now we'll be able to move in at the end of the month,
do you? Mary's got her colors picked out already — she was hoping
you'd mix up those special Simpson pastels for her, if you can spare
the time."

"Sure. Bring her by and we'll get it all down." He looked at the
house, and then down at his schedule. "Yeah, end of the month
should be about right. I got the electrician and the plumber coming
in next week and then the air-conditioning man either Friday or
Monday. After that it's just the plasterers and final touches."

"Good."

"This new carpenter is all right. He's not sloppy. He's coming
back and do all the finish work. That'll probably take a good week,
even with me helping him. Then there's the plaster. So give us a
week, maybe a little more for the fixtures and plates and everything.
Oh yeah, I almost forgot — I got all your fixtures promised from Art
over at the building supply. That tile Mary wanted for the second
bathroom is in the warehouse. Took two weeks to get it."

Beaumont nodded easily, as if he had never given any of this a
second thought from the beginning. *Hey,* Carlyle wanted to say,
*don't think it was easy. Getting all those things the way you want
them takes a lot of hard work.* Beaumont still didn't understand half
of what there was to building a house the way the owner wanted it
built.

"Mary asked me to find out if the wallpaper's in yet."

"That pink stripe? Yeah, it's in." Carlyle groaned. "Harold, you aren't going to let that wife of yours have your bedroom painted pink, too, are you?"

Beaumont's face turned a deeper pink than the wallpaper. "Hell, Carly, I don't know what she's got planned in there. Off-white with maybe a touch of . . . She just wants those colors mixed like you did it in your house."

They walked toward Beaumont's big gold Cadillac with brown velvet seats.

"Well, now, I'll try," Carlyle said. "But you'll have to tell her I won't be able to get the colors just the same. I never have mixed any two yellows exactly alike. You tell her that, will you?"

"Sure, Carly. Don't worry about it. She'll love 'em. So then it's set? I can tell Mary we'll move in around the first of the month."

"Well, like I said, Harold, *if* we don't have any more problems." Then, seeing Beaumont frown, "Oh, sure what the hell. Tell her the first if that's what she wants."

So Mary had seen his house and decided she wanted those pastels for her own place too. Probably thought Helen kept a beautiful home; maybe Helen cleaned it up because someone besides her husband was going to see it. Anyway Mary must have seen the house years ago, because it had been dirty and dingy for a long time now. Everything covered with grease. When Helen mopped a floor it looked dirtier when she finished than it had before she started. Couldn't see a damn thing. And now she was sick.

He hadn't told her that he knew. He just watched her trying to decide when would be a good time to tell him about it.

She did look worse than usual lately, wearing sweaters in the heat . . . And there was that day she had spent in bed. But she said it was only a cold. And the doctor's bill for tests, over a hundred dollars . . . Not that that was unusual for Helen. Always running off for tests. Said she was only a little anemic. Well, why wouldn't he believe her? He had never thought of her as a liar, in addition to everything else.

He heard a noise inside his head like boots crunching on gravel, or small crisp twigs — or maybe a fire crackling. A dry burning without heat. One night he watched her sitting hunched over her knitting, clicking her needles back and forth, stringing different colors of yarn together in patterns she somehow kept in her head. She could remember the number of stitches of this kind and that kind and she would knit special Christmas presents for the children and the nieces in North Carolina. She had been sitting there, half watching television and half knitting, or falling asleep on so many evenings for so many years that it had never occurred to him that a time might come when the rare silences between television shows and commercials would not be punctuated by the dry clicking of her needles.

She waited until the morning that Boatcraft called to tell him the repairs on the boat were finished. She was watching him while he finished breakfast. When the phone rang she answered it.

"That was Boatcraft," she said. "They said you can pick up the boat anytime."

She thought he would be pleased and in a good mood because the boat was ready this soon. But he was thinking of the hundreds of dollars the refinishing would cost, money he had to pay to hide senseless damage done by hateful young punks. Acid rose in his throat like heartburn. He saw the two policemen and Helen and the wet ashes. He looked at her and saw the phony grey-blue sculpture of her hair, her dry lips, the pale nail polish on her bitten nails, the faded housedress. How foolish she was: pouring water on fires, meddling where she shouldn't, trying to look attractive, flabby, wrinkled, shapeless. He gritted his teeth in rage at the shapelessness of her aging woman's body.

"All right," he said quietly, "I'll go pick it up this morning as soon as I get them going at the site. It's the air-conditioning man today, so I can pretty much leave things for a while."

She was quick to jump on this. "Why don't you plan to come home for lunch? I've got that nice leftover roast you liked so much the other night."

Food. That was her weapon. Give him mushy messes half the time, then surprise him with something decent once in a while. She was always thinking about food.

"Just finished breakfast. I can't be bothered thinking about lunch yet."

He walked out, jingling his keys.

He had to shoo some young ones off the site: kids on summer vacation scavenging the piles of discarded lumber, bent rivets, wire and chunks of concrete or things they could sell or use as weapons. When the three boys, aged maybe between eight and ten saw him drive up, they ran to their scattered bicycles, pedals stuck in the sand and sped off. One of them threw back an empty coke bottle. It shattered on the pile of broken concrete.

He parked the car and then cleaned up the broken glass and gathered up some of the trash scattered around — hamburger wrappers, plastic cups and spoons, a white paper bag from a fast food restaurant. He found a few beer cans too. It was par for the course. Build a house anywhere and the neighbors are going to come over to watch it, see what it's made of.

At nine o'clock the air-conditioning man showed up in a big blue van with red and white letters on the side: JOLLY JASPER'S AIR-CONDITIONING AND HEATING, TOTAL CLIMATE CONTROL SYSTEMS FOR THE HOME. Jasper could do the job in two days with one assistant; his competitor had said it would take three days. It didn't matter whether he could spell or not.

Jolly Jasper wasn't laughing this morning, despite the break in the heat which would probably shoot back up to damn near unbearable by noon. It was funny, maybe, when you thought about it: the men who installed air-conditioning units never got to work in air-conditioned comfort; they spent all their time suffering in the heat. And in the winter they froze their hands and ears while they installed heating systems. Maybe that's why Jolly Jasper was so depressed. Well, just so he did his work right. Carlyle watched him get started. He liked the way he hefted large pieces of equipment onto his shoulders and carried them into the house without seeming to feel the weight.

When he came outside he shouted to Carlyle. "Wow *wee*! That's one heck of a house, Mr. Simpson. I heard about it and now I see why. It's real practical the way you did it, two different units."

Carlyle did not smile. He did not want Jasper to know how pleased he was. "Yeah, it's a good design. You see where the two units will handle it all right?"

"Yeah. This big B.T.U. baby goes over there . . . You got it all worked out just right. No problem. We'll have it done by tomorrow night, I reckon."

Carlyle nodded. "Okay, I'll be back."

At Boatcraft they asked him for the money first, when he stepped up to the desk in the front office. The same old story. The receptionist's smile and the smug assistant manager with his fancy office: green carpet and fake wood desk and plastic upholstery on the chairs and ugly panelling. All for show, all to impress customers. He'd rather let the carpet and panelling and secretary go, and deal directly with the man who would do the work.

"No, I'm not ready to pay the bill until I've seen the boat," he told the recptionist. "Where is it?"

Her shiny pink lips stopped smiling. "Oh. Oh well," she said, "just a moment, Mr. Simpson." She got up and went to the door of the office behind her, to ask the assistant manager, she was sorry to disturb him, but Mr. Simpson wanted to see his boat before he paid the bill.

The assistant manager jumped out from behind his desk like a man bitten by ants, and followed the secretary out toward Carlyle. "Of course, Mr. Simpson. I'll take you out to see it now. It's all ready to go." He grinned. "This was a small job, no trouble at all — but we take just as much care with your boat as we do with the cabin cruisers, you can believe me."

Outside, in the lot behind the office, Carlyle saw it and shook his head. Most of the boat was still the sky blue it had always been, but an area nearly a foot in diameter was an ugly blue-green. They had got the dent out all right, but the refinishing was poor.

"That's not what I asked you to do. I said take the dent out and make it look decent. I told you to go ahead and repaint the thing if you had to."

The assistant manager kept grinning. "Oh, come on, Mr. Simpson. We *did* repaint it, can't you see? The uh, uh, repair work on this side affected the way the paint took, that's all. Unavoidable."

"You didn't do it right, then. Don't you people know enough to wait until your undercoat dries before you paint?"

"Now, really, our technicians know what they're doing." The assistant manager stepped back slightly, drawing himself up as though he were as broad-chested as Carlyle, which he was not. "I invite you to take that boat to anybody else and get that work done better for the same price."

Carlyle shook his head again. "You guys *know* you got a fixed market, don't you? But I'll tell you one thing. I ain't paying for no lousy paint job. You do it over."

The assistant manager stopped smiling. "I'm sorry. The work you ordered has been done. If you don't pay for it, you'll have to leave the boat here, and I warn you that if it isn't picked up in thirty days it becomes our property. Pay for this and if you want another paint job, we'll do it. But you'll have to pay for that too."

Carlyle's blood rose thick and fast; he stood with clenched fists watching the man walk back to his office. No way would he let these bastards get more money out of him. But it was clear he was not going to get that boat done without a fight, and he was tired of fighting. He ran his hand across his barely damp forehead and kicked angrily at the rough and pitted pavement.

Then he went back inside and wrote a check for the lousy job and left. Nobody knew anything about workmanship in a place like Boatcraft. Duffy himself would have been the first to say it was just one of those things. Just one of those things, sure. Sure. And he was just a poor old bastard, rooked out of good money by stupid spiteful punks and crooked businessmen. So what else was new? As he left the office, he spat on the doorsill.

Out in the lot he backed his car up to the boat and its trailer. He got out and hitched it painfully, letting it drop into place with a jerk, hooking the chains so violently they tore into the scab where the hook had cut his hand. He did not bother to see if it was bleeding; he just drove away.

Helen came out to the driveway while he was unhitching the boat. "Did Bob say anything to you about Sarah coming?" She thought she was approaching him while he was still in a good mood about getting his boat back. Naturally she wouldn't notice the two different paint colors.

"Yeah, I guess he said something about it."

"I imagine she'll be staying here for a little while."

"Hmm." The scab had torn off and there was blood in his palm. "When is she supposed to be coming?"

"The first of next week." She was watching him anxiously. "She's going to be keeping house, Carlyle. The doctors want me in the hospital for a few days." She began to talk more quickly. "It's just for some tests, but they say it's absolutely necessary. Maybe a week. I wouldn't do it if—"

"You didn't tell me you were sick," he said.

Her face flushed a dull red. "Well, I didn't—I didn't want to—worry you . . ."

"No," he said. "I'm the last to know. You don't tell me anything. Oh, sure. Sure. Put you in the hospital, what do they care? All they want is their money."

Her face was still red and now she raised her voice. Helen was not herself. "You know darn well the insurance will pay for it," she said loudly. "I don't know why you have to be so nasty about everything all the time. You're just plain nasty, Carlyle Simpson, that's what you are, and I'm sick of it. You act as if I *want* to go to the hospital. You think I'm going to *enjoy* it?" She turned away and did not seem to care whether he threw something at her or went after her. "I'm going in on Sunday, whatever you do, and that's that. Sarah's coming to take care of you, and you don't have to take me if you don't want to. Just do whatever you want."

"Sure," he mumbled. "Sure." He watched her go into the house. He was too tired to move.

The Beaumont house had clean lines, and nestled on the lot as though someone who cared about it had set it down just exactly where it was supposed to be, near the best pine shade trees left on the lot. And just the right distance from the road. Carlyle could imagine the lawn, sodded thickly with Argentine Bahaia, sloping gently down to the curb like the manicured hills at Townsend Country Club: gentle, soft green.

But now the sandy lot was littered with stray boards. In the bright sun it looked almost like a child's large sandbox and the house like a playhouse. He went inside where Jolly Jasper and his assistant were doing his rough-in and installing the ducts. Carlyle smiled when he saw the pink bathtub in Beaumont's master bath. The plumber had sent it the other day, just the tubs and pipes, no other fixtures had been roughed in. The second bathroom had a blue tub. Mary Beaumont would probably want either one or both of the guest bedrooms painted blue. The day after Mortimer came back to do the finish work, the tile man would come in to do the shower in the third bathroom, and all the tile. Blue floral tile in the second bath, yellow floral in the third bath. Yellow floral on a white background, and he could bet that Mary Beaumont would keep it clean too.

Jolly Jasper was moving quickly along; he would be finished by the next afternoon. The insulation was coming in the day after that; fiberglas for the ceiling and inside walls and styrofoam on the outside walls. Then the plasterers and the finish work, the cabinet man, the tile man and the last of the plumbing and electrical plates and fixtures. The electrician had used copper wiring; while Carlyle was retired everyone had switched back from aluminum to copper again. Just like the new window regulations: you had to have one in every bedroom for fire protection. He shook his head. Always some kind of a new rule to keep a contractor busy and give him trouble.

The last jobs were the painting and the exterior finish, the stucco. He would do the painting himself, since that was what Mary Beaumont wanted. She was a smart woman. She knew he had the best eye and would do the most careful, the neatest job. Maybe this was a house worth building, a house that would be taken care of. Scovill hadn't been able to ruin it; neither had the amateurs at the building supply or the punks with their coke bottles.

Beaumont had paid him his second draw and would give him the third in less than two weeks. He was beginning to believe that Beaumont was going to get his money's worth after all. There

weren't many buyers who would spend thousands of dollars more
than the going rate for a subdivision house; but there weren't many
buyers nowadays who would get a house as well built as this one. It
was pleasant standing in the cool empty living room, listening to the
air-conditioning men installing the metal pieces: there was a hol-
lowness in a newly built house unlike any other, and everything
sounded different in these rooms now from the way it would sound
once the carpets were down and the walls were painted and the
drapes were hung. Soon there would be furniture and clutter. But
for nearly two more weeks this would be a clean space where you
could stand and listen to the sounds of men working, the only
sounds worth hearing.

NINE

THE SOUND OF PASCAGOULI'S HAMMER

On Sunday he took Helen to the hospital and deposited her. Another thing he had to worry with. Now he had a house to finish. Bob was meeting Sarah at the airport so he could stay at the site. The plasterers were there; they planned to work late so they could finish up. He could still remember the days when there was no high-grade lime for quick drying, and the plasterers had used horse-hair. Now they used the rock lathe method, three good coats, an extra half inch of plaster in all, and you could paint in a few days. Mistakes in the wood could be covered by the plasterers, but Carlyle took pleasure in knowing that there were few mistakes in the wood in this house. The plaster in this house didn't have to hide anything.

When he left the Beaumont house, he was tired. He stopped at Johnny's to have a few and then he suddenly remembered that Sarah was home. Nelson tried to get him to stay and arm-wrestle, but he said he didn't feel like bothering with it. He had had a long, hard day and he had to get on home.

Sarah was sitting in the living room in Helen's chair, watching television. When she saw him standing in the doorway she smiled and got up. "Hi, Pop," she said, and hugged him.

"Been a long time, huh?" he said.

He went into the kitchen to see what there was to eat. It was straightened up; the dishes were washed and there was nothing on the stove. She followed him.

"I didn't keep dinner waiting. I didn't know when you'd get here and it would get all dried out."

He hadn't seen her for two years. Her yellow hair was tucked behind her ears, probably because of the heat. She had always hated Florida summers. She was wearing a pair of cut-off blue jeans and an old T-shirt, but at least she seemed to be wearing a bra. Maybe she always did. She did look older. Her manner was calm and friendly. She didn't seem annoyed that he had come home so late for dinner.

"So would you like me to fix you a steak? I can heat up the vegetables. I only put them away about an hour ago. You didn't have dinner out, did you?"

He shook his head.

"Well, it will only take a few minutes. The newspaper's in the living room if you want to look at it."

So he sat in the living room, as he almost never did, skimming the dull news in the paper. Red tide was driving the tourists from the beaches again this summer. He read a couple of letters to the editor. The same old guy from one of the trailer parks who wrote in every few days about some stupid problem or about nothing, just to see his name in print. This one was some kind of attack on the county commission. Carlyle put the paper down. He was really tired. When his dinner was ready, he ate quickly, said goodnight to Sarah and went back to his bedroom.

Pascagouli's hammer drove home each of the small nails on the trim in a series of well-aimed blows. Yesterday, with Bob's help, he had hung the doors. The plasterers were finished. Today Pascagouli was going to put in the moldings and the baseboard, and the chair rail in the living room, dining room and foyer. It was the hottest day of the summer so far; inside the nearly completed house the air was thick and moist. Carlyle's undershirt was barely damp.

"It's the damned humidity," Bob said. He was carrying lengths of baseboard from Pascagouli's sawhorses in the middle of the living room to the corner where he was nailing them carefully into place, working much more slowly than Pascagouli.

"Yes," Pascagouli said. "I feel like a sponge that ought to be wrung."

"We're soaked already," Bob said, "and it's not even eleven o'clock."

But Carlyle felt too dry. He thought wryly that if anyone were to touch him they would receive a shock. He looked at the baseboard: it was wider and thicker—and more expensive—than most baseboards; it would make the house look more solid, distinctive. People would notice these baseboards and they would know this was a Simpson house.

The sound of regular hammer blows stopped while Pascagouli measured and cut more baseboard. Bob's halting, irregular blows continued.

"Hey Pop," Bob called suddenly. "How was Mom last night? How's it going?"

Carlyle pretended not to hear. Pascagouli went on measuring and cutting. Carlyle liked that: although the carpenter talked a lot, he didn't seem nosy.

"How was she?" Bob said. He stopped hammering and looked at Carlyle. "Didn't you go to see Mom last night?"

"No, I didn't," Carlyle said shortly. He was annoyed that Bob would bring this up in front of Pascagouli. "Sarah went by herself. I was tired."

"Oh." A pause. "Well, I'm going tonight if you want to come with me."

Shut up, Carlyle thought, *you know I hate hospitals.* "Nah," he said. "Not tonight, don't think so anyway . . . Listen, looks like you two might be finishing this damn place up today and it *is* just about the hottest day of the year—what say we all three go have a few cold ones together at Johnny's as soon as we're done?" He added, "That is, of course, if Mr. Pascagouli is free to join us."

Bob just looked at him. Sore about Helen. Damn it, there was nothing wrong with her. She was just in for tests and they wouldn't find anything. She was getting old, that was all.

"Well," Pascagouli said uncertainly, looking from one to the other. "I don't . . ."

"Okay," Carlyle said quickly. "That's okay. Don't worry about it. If you guys are busy, just forget about it."

They worked in silence after that.

Carefully, taking his time, Carlyle put up the chair rail in the dining room. The elegant baseboards, the chair rail, the moldings on the doors—people would admire them, but they wouldn't know how solid the foundation and walls were, beneath the decoration. But *he* knew it.

Pascagouli was bending over his moldings like an old lady clucking over her grandchildren. A black harness-strap kept his glasses on his head, his greasy black hair with its sprinkling of sawdust stuck out wildly between that and the dirty white terry cloth sweatband. Even Bob, with his long hair, looked neater. Pascagouli was big and loose and sloppy but he was a precise craftsman. It was hard to believe that he had worked as a carpenter summers only for the past eight years. It would really be something if Bob could learn from him. But it seemed to be a natural gift, and Carlyle did not think Bob had it in him.

When they finished everything, including the built-in shelves in the closets and the pantry, the house smelt freshly of sawdust and wood shavings. Carlyle swept each room, and gathered up the shavings and dust into large bags that had held boxes of nails and such like, and took them outside. He tried all the doors that had been planed and hung the day before: each one cleared the floor with exactly the right extra space needed for carpeting, except for the closets, pantry and bathrooms where there would be no carpet. The doors were all wood. No masonite in *this* house.

They stood waiting for him in the driveway, their chests and arms streaked with dirt, their jeans, even with the brown belts, hanging loose around their hips. When Carlyle came out, they were dusting the shavings and sawdust from their pants and wriggling into their shirts. Carlyle paid them. But they still stood there. He was waiting for them to leave.

Pascagouli took the sweat-soaked terry cloth band off his head and wrung it out hard. "Now how about those cold ones?" he said to Carlyle.

For in an instant, just before they opened the door to go in, Carlyle felt a sharp pang of regret that he had invited them. He hated to think what Johnny and Nelson—and Vicki too—would think of the two of them.

When Vicki came to the table, he said, "Vicki, can you bring three of the biggest coldest beers you got—draft Bud for me, and whatever these gentlemen prefer—draft Bud for everybody?— okay, just as soon as you can. This here's my son Bob—I know he needs a haircut—and this here's Mr. Mortimer Pascagouli, the best trim carpenter anywhere in this county."

The air was cold as autumn, but it was stale. He wished he was out on the Gulf in a good strong wind.

Vicki brought the beers. "So you're old Carly's boy, are you?" she said, just as sweet as she could with her southern twang, treating Bob like he was special. "Don't you think your daddy's too hard on you young fellas with the hair? Carlyle Simpson, you got a fine-lookin' young-un and you oughta be proud of him. And I guess maybe you are." She winked at Bob. "Betcha didn't know your mean old daddy here brags about you behind your back."

"Vicki," Carlyle said, "don't go givin' this boy a swelled head." He liked her even when she talked too much. Bob had turned pink. He sipped his beer; it was obvious the kid didn't drink often.

"You know, Dad," Bob said, when they were sitting over menus, "Mort here worked with Ben Starritt."

"No kiddin'," Carlyle said. It was a small world.

"Yes," Pascagouli said, "one summer. He was pretty old then, but he was a fine carpenter." He took a long drink of beer and settled back in his chair, stretching his legs far beneath the table to the rungs on the empty chair opposite him. "I found out I liked working with wood that summer. And another summer I worked with Mr. Scovill . . ." He shook his head. "We worked on that Pine Lakes subdivision . . ."

Carlyle wrinkled his nose. "I know who built that," he said. "Don't even mention that bastard's name."

"I feel the same way," Pascagouli said. "It was a bad summer. I can imagine that you and Mr. Scovill wouldn't get along, Mr. Simpson. He's not a craftsman. He threw a few nails in each board — that was all right with the builder. Mr. Scovill really wasn't interested in his work; he wanted to get home to his wife and baby. Well." He took a reflective drink. "Of course the baby was sick . . . Well, he was recovering. But he had a rare form of cancer . . ."

There was an awkward silence. Carlyle tried to imagine Scovill confiding his sorrows to Pascagouli. Bob was looking at his watch. "Listen, Pop," he said, "don't you think —"

"Hey, you know what?" Carlyle said. "We'd better order some dinner. How about it? It's on me. The hamburgers aren't bad here."

"Say, Pop, listen, don't you think Sarah will be expecting you home for dinner? Maybe we could call her up and ask her to meet us here and eat with us. She won't have to bother with dinner and then we can all go over to the hospital together. Shall I call her? I know we look kind of gungy today, but that won't bother Sarah."

"It's not a good idea," Carlyle said. "Forget it."

"Well, but listen Pop, Mort and Sarah haven't seen each other for about four years. You'd like to see her, wouldn't you, Mort?"

Carlyle felt his blood rising; his skull seemed to tighten painfully.

"I said *no*, dammit!"

It came out louder than he had intended; chairs squeaked behind him as people turned to look. He hated the look on Bob's face. The kid never could handle loud voices or arguments. He always cried too much and never fought enough. Carlyle took a deep breath, and tried to speak softly.

"This ain't the place for Sarah. I'm not bringing any daughter of mine in here, and that's that. I don't want her in a place like this." If he could only get through to Bob — he was his son; the same blood pulsed in both their veins. That had to be worth something.

Bob hesitated, still leaning forward. "Well, I'll be damned," he said. "But what about Vicki? You don't object to her working here, do you?"

"That's not the same thing."

"Oh Pop, listen, Sarah's twenty-five years old now. She's a grown woman. Why, you don't know where she goes . . . I mean, it's so old-fashioned —"

"All right, then. You call her. Let her come here and embarrass me, who cares," Carlyle said bitterly. "Shit, maybe I'll just go along. We damn near finished building a house today and I thought maybe the three of us could have a few beers and a hamburger and relax. It's the last day on the trim. Oh, what the hell." He stirred a little puddle of beer on the table with his finger. "What's the damned use, anyway?"

There was another awkward silence.

"Well, okay," Bob said. "Why don't I just call and tell her you won't be home for dinner." He went off to the pay phone.

"So," Pascagouli said. "The owners will be moving in next week?"

"Yeah. Tomorrow the cabinet man comes, and the day after that the tile man. Then the plumber and electrician finish up on Thursday. That's when the juice gets turned on."

"They seem like nice people . . . the owners."

"Yeah, Beaumont. You know him? He used to be on the school board."

Pascagouli shook his head. "No, I never heard of him before I worked on his house."

That was good, Pascagouli thinking of the house as Beaumont's house. That was the way it should be. When you worked construction, you should always keep the individual owners in mind. Subdivision contractors didn't do that; half the time they didn't know or care who they were building for.

Bob came back and they ordered dinner.

"So what's your next job, Mort?" Carlyle asked. He was surprised to hear himself ask the question, and to hear himself calling Pascagouli by his first name. "What do you have planned?"

"Well, I'm thinking about moving back up north. I've saved a little money. I'd like to build a cabin in New England. I'm going to look around up in Maine."

"Maine? What in hell you going to do up there?"

Before Pascagouli could answer, Bob jumped in.

"What's wrong with Maine? There's nothing wrong with Maine. You've never even been there."

Carlyle ignored him. Pascagouli looked embarrassed, or as close to embarrassed as a man like Pascagouli could look.

"Well, it's pretty up there. And I guess I'll do the same thing in Maine that I'd do in Tennessee or here or anywhere. I don't like cities much, but otherwise I'm not sure it makes that much difference where you live."

If anyone else had given him an answer like that, Carlyle would have been ready to belt him one. But Pascagouli was different. He was sincere, you could feel it. And you could feel something else about him: he seemed kind of sad. Not depressed, but there was a sadness about him that was hard to pin down. But it drew Carlyle to him, this oddball who was educated but who knew what hard work was.

"I really would like to leave Florida," Pascagouli went on. "I need a change. Maybe I'll find out there is no real change, but I want to try it. How about you, Mr. Simpson? Do you ever feel that you'd like to try some place new?"

Carlyle shrugged. It had never entered his head to leave Florida. But he had certainly wanted a change when he left Carolina.

"I don't know," he said. "I like this warm weather. I hated shovelling snow. I moved here on account of that, and I thought I'd do a lot of golf and fish. It wasn't so crowded down here when I came. It was a lot nicer. Now it seems like all the tourists want to move down here for good." He didn't want to go on and talk about his back trouble and all that; that had finished off the golf, anyway.

Bob wolfed down his second hamburger. The kid had a good appetite, even though he was so damn skinny. He looked at his watch again.

"Hey, Pop, are you coming to the hospital? Visiting hours are over early."

Carlyle gathered his response carefully. "Nah, you go by yourself tonight. She'll enjoy seeing the two of you. I'll go some other time." *If I feel like it.* He rested his scabbed hand on the cool dark Formica.

"Well, Mort," Bob said, "let's get together some time before you head north. Maybe before Sarah goes back, huh?"

Pascagouli smiled. "Sure," he said. "We'll see." Carlyle remembered suddenly that Mort was Sarah's friend. He wasn't anxious to see her again, that was obvious.

"Okay, I'll call you tomorrow. Thanks for the beers and for dinner, Pop," he added half-heartedly.

Carlyle shrugged off the thanks. "Listen," he said, "you got another job this week?"

"No. Why?"

"Well, you know, Mary Beaumont wants me to do the painting, and I guess I could use some help, if you'd like to try. I'll be ready to do the primer on Wednesday or Thursday. I could use you Thursday and Friday for sure."

"Are you sure? I know how particular you are."

Carlyle turned to Pascagouli. "See that? Pay the kid a compliment, and already he's suspicious." He gave a dry chuckle. "Listen, I can get somebody else. I just thought it would be a good chance for you to learn more about that end of things. House painters make pretty good money, you know. You got a good eye and a steady hand. I could give you a few tips."

Bob hesitated.

"Pay you carpenters' wages. How about it?" He couldn't believe this hesitation. He was doing the kid a favor.

"Okay," Bob said slowly. "I'll come in Thursday morning. Should I bring anything?"

"Nah. I'll take care of everything."

"All right, I'm on my way. Anything you want me to tell Mom?"

"Yeah," Carlyle said. Bob looked surprised. "Tell her to hurry up and get the hell out of there. Every day she's there those doctors charge more money for nothing."

Bob's face darkened; he left without another word.

Carlyle ordered one more round for the road.

"How about you, Mr. Simpson?" Pascagouli asked. "What are *your* plans? What will you do after this house is finished?"

Carlyle ran his hand over his chin and thought. He knew he would get his lawn back in shape. He might do a lot of things. Or maybe he wouldn't do anything. There were no more houses to build, that was for sure.

"Oh," he said, "I guess I'll do a little fishing. Pretty soon I'll be playing shuffleboard with the old codgers in Trailer Heaven. I ain't getting any younger, you know."

Pascagouli looked surprised. "You mean you're not building anything else right away?"

"Right away? Hell, I'm finished. I'll never build anything else. Hey, I retired ten years ago, you know, retired from the business. This was just a favor for Harold Beaumont. The last Simpson house." He banged his scabbed palm softly on the table. "No, thanks," he said emphatically. "I don't need it any more, not with all the cheap bastards in the business, all out to cheat you. And carpenters . . . why, you're the last one, and you're moving away." He laughed bitterly. "Lazy. Don't want to work. Don't even know how."

"Well," Pascagouli said. He looked upset. "Bob — ?"

"Oh, he's done all right. But he won't stick to it. He's going to run off one of these days, going to get tired of it. He's going to look for something easier." He suddenly felt very sad, and took a deep drink of beer. *Not like the old man.*

"You can't be sure," Pascagouli said. He looked at Carlyle suddenly. "But won't you be awfully *bored*?" he asked intently.

"Bored?" That wasn't a word Carlyle used. "I can't say about that. I can't say I've ever been bored."

"Why, that's wonderful," Pascagouli said. "But with no more houses to build . . . And you're a builder, Mr. Simpson." He leaned across the table toward Carlyle. "Pardon my intrusion," he said, "but for God's sake don't play a little shuffleboard and do a little fishing. Don't let it happen."

"What do you mean? Don't let *what* happen?" The blood began to pound in his temples.

"Whatever it is — whatever is happening to you . . ."

Carlyle stood up.

"It's been a pleasure to work with you, Mr. Pascagouli. It's getting late." He stared coldly past the younger man and did not put his hand out.

Pascagouli began to rise, like a big frightened bear. Carlyle walked out, sorry to leave him.

TEN

BENEATH
THE SURFACE

The next morning Carlyle went out to a restaurant for breakfast before Sarah got up. It was one of those shiny chains that served defrosted potatoes instead of grits. But at least the dishes and silverware were nice and clean, and the eggs were not greasy. He felt thirsty and drank glass after glass of water without satisfaction.

After he ate he went over to the house to watch the cabinet man get started. He had to make sure the man allowed for clearance on the dishwasher when he set in the drawers. In subdivision homes more often than not two or three of the kitchen drawers were unusable because the stupid man hadn't thought about clearance for doors and drawers near appliances. It was horrible to think of building a house perfectly level, plumb and square and then having some cabinetman ruin it with sloppy work everyone could see, and that would cause inconvenience every day for the people who lived there.

The kitchen was the most important room in the house. At least it was for the women, so he was not surprised when Mary Beaumont drove up and walked into her new house to see exactly what the cabinetman was doing with her cabinets in her kitchen.

"Why, hel-*lo*, Mr. Simpson," she said. She was beaming with excitement.

Now that the house was completed, he did not object to her being there. The site was no place for women, although Bob would probably disagree with that. He would probably love to work with those young women who were being hired to work construction in some parts of the country. But no woman had ever worked construction for Carlyle Simpson, and no woman ever would.

Mary Beaumont sparkled. She was still an attractive woman; no wonder Harold let her have her own way on interior decorating. Her long wavy hair was dark red, almost brown, darker than auburn. Maybe she dyed it, but so what? It looked good. It was certainly better than that old lady blue. That was probably supposed to be "respectable"; they could feel superior to women who dyed their hair "young" colors. But it was all hiding just the same.

"Well, Mr. Simpson, I must say—"

"Cut that out, Mary. I'm 'Carlyle' to you and you know it."

She smiled. "All right, Carlyle. You certainly have done a remarkable job here. Harold and I were over the other night; we were both really impressed with everything. It's all those little extra details . . . that beautiful floor in the foyer . . . It's all exactly what we wanted, it's exactly the way we hoped it would be."

He kept his face muscles in control. He didn't want to let himself be flattered by this striking woman, but he couldn't help enjoying it. The cabinet man knew he was enjoying it too.

"Harold always said you were the best in the business, and he certainly knew what he was talking about. There's not a new house in this town—I mean the really expensive ones—that can hold a candle to this one. It's worth every cent—really it's *cheap* for what it is."

Carlyle did not meet her blue eyes directly. "Well, I do think you got yourself a house here."

"Soon as it's painted and decorated I want to have a party. You and Helen have to come. Now about the painting—I want you to take your time. I know it's a big job. I hope you're not planning to get it done all by yourself before next Tuesday."

"Well . . ."

"Now why don't you take your time and do the guest bedrooms after we've moved in? We won't be ready to unpack *everything* right away, and I don't mind your company for a little while." She threw back her head and laughed. She seemed much younger than fifty. Her figure was almost as trim as Sarah's and he liked her clothes. Her dark rust cotton suit nearly matched her hair, and the collar of her delicate print blouse was open, setting off her fine bones.

She put her hand on his arm. He felt a kind of current run all the way to his shoulder. "Listen, I know we've given you a hard time. Here you were, trying to enjoy the retired life and Harold and I come along and drag you out to build a house, and now I'm forcing you to come paint it for us. But I hope you know that I wouldn't be asking if it wasn't important to me. I know you're the only one who can do it just right."

Carlyle stepped back slightly, to move his arm away from her hand. It was a lovely hand with carefully tended rosy nails, and it fell at once to her side. "Now that you're here," he said, "why don't we talk about it?"

He went out and got the book of tints from his car.

They went through the rooms one by one, and he showed her how he could vary each tine — darken it or lighten it, or mix it with something to make it warmer or cooler, and he made some notes. In the end she said she wanted Carlyle to use his own judgment on each tint. She said she trusted his eye a whole lot better than she trusted her own. She put her hand on his arm again when she said that, and looked up at him with her trusting blue eyes.

At the front door, just before she left, she said, "Now Carlyle, honey, don't forget to give my best to Helen." She leaned over and kissed his cheek. "And thanks for everything again," she said softly.

He watched her cross the street and get into her car.

He got the paints and for the rest of the afternoon he mixed his colors in the Beaumont garage. He used bases and colorants for the pale shades of yellow, beige, pink and blue that he wanted, variations from the manufacturer's stock shades. Some of the tints were so pale that people might mistake them for white until they realized that the walls were subtly picking up the colors of the upholstery. He mixed carefully and made samples of two shades of each color that would dry overnight so he could compare them tomorrow. He never used latex paint; it did not hide imperfections or wash as well as alkyd or other old-fashioned paints. He finished and cleaned his natural hog bristle brushes by soaking them in mineral spirits. Tomorrow he would start the primer. Bob would help on Thursday and by Friday he could begin the finish coats. He thought he had better finish by Tuesday.

"Give my best to Helen," Mary Beaumont had said, and much as he hated hospitals, here he was, taking the elevator to her floor, walking down the gleaming, ugly corridor, his shoes clacking with a

metallic echo. Three beds to a room here, and everything from old
dried-up prunes who looked as if they'd been dead for years, to kids
who had no business being in a place like this. Most likely they were
the ones who were really sick.

Nurses passed him; in their white uniforms they looked like
lifeless cotton dolls; and the corridor smelled lifeless, too, chemical,
antiseptic. No honest sweat here. He was still thirsty. He stopped at
every drinking fountain and took long gulps.

She was propped up on pillows, looking at a magazine. One of
the beds was empty, and a small lady with white hair sat on the third
one, talking away. When she saw Carlyle, she said, "Is that yours,
honey?" and bounced off the bed as though she didn't belong in any
hospital. "I'll just go for a little walk and leave you alone."

Helen put down the magazine. She looked tired, but not as bad
as those dried prunes, anyway. He sat down on a straight chair.

"So what do they say?" he asked her. Might as well get to the
point. "What'd they find out from the tests?"

She looked away from him, to the window. It was dirty, but he
could see a few run-down buildings through it. Doctors' offices,
insurance agencies. These Florida doctors, these Florida towns,
they seemed to exist just to cheat old people out of their money. A
lot of people came to Florida to die.

"They don't know anything so far," she said. "Dr. Owens says I'll
probably be here until Monday or Tuesday. They haven't been able
to find out what it is."

"And now you're more weak and tired than ever from the tests,
right? Boy, they really like to put you through things." He felt sorry
for her, because she looked sick and because they wouldn't tell her
anything about it.

"They haven't really been too bad, most of them. But I'll be glad
when it's over."

There was a vase of flowers on her nightstand and some flowers
and a plant on a shelf near the window. He pointed his chin at them.
"Those yours?"

She followed his eyes. "Oh, yes. People have certainly been
thoughtful."

"Mary Beaumont sends you her best."

"Mary Beaumont? How did she know? Did you tell her?"

"No. She just came by the house—their house. They're moving in next week. It's finished. Before she left she said to give you her best. I didn't tell her anything. Got no time to stand around telling people things."

"Oh. Well, that's nice of her anyway."

Yeah, he thought. She's nice all right.

"I guess she's got you wrapped around her little finger by now," Helen said unexpectedly. "She'll get you to knock yourself out to get that house all finished for her. She knows how to get around men."

Startled, he lost his temper.

"Oh, shut up," he said, violently. "What do you know about it? You don't know squat. I'm a contractor, remember? I got a schedule to follow, and I damn well better follow it, and keep my customers satisfied. *Nobody* who ever bought a Simpson house was *ever* disappointed. You'd like to see me mess it up, wouldn't you? Well, that damned house is going to be done on time and done *right*." He paused, out of breath. She lay there looking yellow and drawn. "Don't you ever try to tell me not to get my work done on time!" he said, dropping his voice. "You can stay here and vacation all you want."

"I'm just worried about you," Helen said. "You don't know how to relax, you never have. You always overdo. That's all."

He waited for her to go on. Maybe she would start talking about his drinking next. He still felt angry. "Well, don't tell me how to do things," he said sullenly. "Hell, *you're* the one in the hospital."

She lay back on the pillows and closed her eyes.

He got up and walked over to the window.

"Sarah been fixing your dinners all right?" she asked.

A dump truck had smashed the bumper on a little sports car. The fat truck driver and the skinny teenage boy were standing in the street yelling at each other.

"Sarah's all right," he said.

"Bob told me you asked him to help you with the painting," she said. "That really meant a lot to him, Carlyle."

"Yeah, well. He may be all right and then again he may not. I'll see. I'll tell you one thing: I'm not going to let some damn kid ruin my house."

She didn't answer. He turned from the window to look at her and saw that she was crying. Tears were streaking across her cheek to her neck.

He cleared his throat, although it was dry and scratchy, and stood there, looking at her and jingling his keys in his pocket.

"You got a pain?" he asked uncertainly after a while.

"Not some damn kid," she said. Her voice was muffled.

"Not what?"

"He's not some damn kid," she said. "He was so . . . pleased . . . you asked him." She gave a strangled sob and sat up to take a tissue from the box on the table next to her. She blew her nose. Her eyes were red in her white face, her grey hair was awry. "I think you hate us all," she whispered. "I'm scared, Carlyle, I'm sick and I'm scared." She wept again for a moment. "And I'm scared for you. I wish I wasn't, but I am."

"Don't need you to worry about me," he mumbled.

"Oh, I know," she said. "I know you don't."

"Damn right I don't." Rage flooded into him; why was she saying these things? What was the point?

She lay back again, and closed her eyes.

"Oh, why can't you let anything go, ever?" she said in a low voice. "I wish you'd leave. I don't know why you came."

He was leaving all right. He looked out the window again, trying to think of something to say. A highway patrolman was breaking up the argument between the teenager and the truck driver. It had almost turned into a fight. The road was cleared and traffic moved on again, back almost to a normal flow, every isolated driver hating every other driver taking up space on the road.

The smell of the alkyd paint filled the air, spreading like the pale primer covering the white plaster. He had the windows wide open.

On Thursday Bob came and Carlyle showed him the rooms he had already done, ignoring the plumber and the electrician who were still at work. Carlyle explained that it was important to watch the doorways, where too many painters slopped the paint over the baseboard, which in this house would be painted white in all the rooms. Or they slopped the white paint from the baseboard and moldings over onto the wall—just a bit here and a bit there. The painter might not even notice it at the time. But it would be there. A mistake.

"Maybe you better do all the tricky parts," Bob said nervously.

"Well, let's see how you do on the wall flat. If you can keep the roller and the brushes from touching the ceiling you'll be all right. Use all the masking tape you need, but use it right."

He climbed the stepladder and showed Bob how to line up the tape so that when it was removed the paint line would end at the exact point where wall and ceiling met.

Bob watched him with wide eyes. "You don't even need to use the tape half the time, do you?" he asked.

"I can see a straight line and keep it with this little brush," Carlyle said. "I got to keep a steady hand, that's all." He showed Bob the different paint brushes; six inch wall flats and smaller ones with rounded, flat and slanted edges.

"I can see this isn't going to be the way I painted my apartment," Bob said.

"Better not be."

He started Bob using the primer in one of the guest bedrooms; he told him to be careful not to get paint on the plates, which the electrician had just finished installing, or the fixtures. Then Carlyle began on the living room: the primer was dry there and the electrician had finished that room too. The living room was going to be a pale beige, almost an off white. He painted easily for a couple of hours, enjoying it and feeling relaxed. Then he thought he had better check on Bob. As he stepped slowly off the stepladder, he felt pain in his back for the first time that day. That was the worst thing about painting. Before he was finished, his back would be giving him more and more trouble. He would just have to move real slow getting on and off the ladder and be careful about reaching. No way he could afford to wind up in traction. No hospital was going to get *him*.

Bob was standing in the guest room rubbing his fingers. When he saw his father he smiled his nervous smile. "My hands aren't used to this. Even after all the work I've been doing. Using these different handles gets to you after a while. Doesn't it?"

"I don't reckon it will hurt you none. If you get a blister you can stop." He saw that Bob had done very little. "You can work faster, can't you?"

"Oh, sure, I'll try and speed up." He went on rubbing his fingers. "Say, what about that cut on your hand? I noticed it the other night. Doesn't it bother you while you're painting?"

The scab had finally broken halfway off and left good skin.

"It's healing all right."

"Hey, isn't that good news about Mom coming home? The doctors don't think it's cancer or anything like that."

"Yeah," Carlyle said. "We got work to do." He left the room.

Later he went to look at the bathroom fixtures the plumber had just installed. Everything seemed nice and neat, but the faucet handles were reversed in the master bathroom. Who wanted to turn the H handle and get cold water, and be scalded when they turned the C handle? Damn. You had to breathe down their goddam necks every goddam minute. This plumber had worked for him before. He ought to know better. He found the man in the driveway, with his head poked inside his van.

"Hey, you ain't going off and leavin' those fixtures like that! Get back in there and do that master bath over!"

The man pulled his head out of the van.

"What's up your nose this time, Simpson? Who do you think you're talkin' to, some kid?" He got his things together and followed Carlyle back to the house. In the master bath Carlyle pointed to the faucets.

"You ain't gettin' by with this kind of thing here. You do them right, and then you'll get paid."

"Jeez," the man grumbled, "you don't have to get so damn riled up." But he started to loosen the handles.

Oh, it *burned* him. They were all trying to get away with something, every last one of them. He stood on the stepladder, using the narrow brush, painting the straightest line anyone could want along the edge of the ceiling. He didn't need masking tape to hide the ceiling; he'd keep that brush exactly where it was supposed to be. Steady, even strokes, not too hard, not too soft, with just the right amount of paint on the brush. No dripping, no spattering. The smell of paint was strong in his nostrils, and anger burned in his stomach and his throat. His back and neck were stiff and sore. He could not forget that they were all out to cheat him, one way or another. All the rest of that day he kept thinking about Scovill, about Eyebrows at Johnny's, about the assistant manager at Boatcraft. And now the stupid plumber, wasting time, wasting money.

He finished the living room before Bob had the primer coat on the smallest bedroom. He drank all the ice water in his thermos; he was terribly thirsty. Then he drove to a convenience store, bought a carton of lemonade and drank that too. He came back, ready to start on the dining room, but when he saw how slowly Bob was moving, he decided to finish up the primer in the other guest bedroom. All his muscles and joints felt sore, but he painted vigorously, barely managing to finish the bedroom by the time it grew too dark to see.

Bob had finished only the one bedroom. So far at least he had not ruined it. Putting the finish coat on tomorrow would be the acid test. Carlyle went into the new kitchen, with its clean, shiny cabinets gleaming in the half-light, the Formica countertops looking smooth as glass. In a few days it would all be changed. Mary Beaumont would have her dishes and things in the cabinets; as soon as the refrigerator was delivered she'd be putting food into it. The kitchen would never be a disaster like Helen's but it would never again be as clean as it was now. There would be one day — maybe after he finished painting it — when he would want everyone to see the kitchen and the whole house. But after that it would be different. Then the house wouldn't be his any more.

It would belong to the Beaumonts. And it probably meant about as much to Beaumont as his Cadillac did. He just wanted to brag that he had the best contractor in town, and the best of everything. He didn't really understand; he hadn't really seen what went into it. And look at that plumber. But who cared? It didn't seem to make any difference to people whether things were done right or wrong. They just wanted everything to look nice and to work.

And here he'd gone and made a fool of himself, trying to get people to do things the way he knew they should be done. And none of them cared. Except Pascagouli. Carlyle was conscious of the sour taste in his mouth and the burning in his stomach. He was thirsty again. He wished he had not said what he had said to Pascagouli, but there was not a damn thing he could do about it now. "Whatever it is, don't just let it happen," the guy had said. Whatever it was. He walked to his car through the hot August air, thick as fog.

The next day he put Bob to work on the finish coat over the dried primer. The bedrooms were the easiest, so he let Bob keep the smallest bedroom. "Make sure you cover every inch of primer and not an inch of ceiling!"

The man from the power company turned on the electricity and the wallpaper man came to do the bathrooms and part of the kitchen. Carlyle checked to see that he hung the right paper. He'd heard too many cases of owners walking in and finding a paper that they had never ordered on the walls. The man carried the roll of pink stuff into the master bath. Carlyle could not help smiling. Maybe he would put up with pink wallpaper, too, if he was married to Mary Beaumont. But he didn't much like the idea of being married to *her,* either. A night or two, maybe a week. After that, it would get old fast. Even with her.

By noon Bob had finished only a couple of walls. Carlyle stood in the doorway and watched. Bob was dripping with sweat; the back of his faded T-shirt was dark with it. Carlyle looked at the wall and shook his head.

"I'll be damned," he said.

Bob turned, startled. "Huh?"

"Give me that stepladder." He carried it in one hand, grimacing at the strain on his back. He set it down again on the tarpaulin and climbed up three steps to look at the line where the ceiling met the wall. He had already seen it from the doorway.

"See that?"

"What?"

"This isn't straight. Can't you see it with your own eyes? This isn't straight. You've got blue going over the line here."

Bob squinted up at the ceiling, trying to see the flaw. It was clear that he couldn't see it.

"Looks all right to me. It's such a pale color, it's just a little bluer than the ceiling." His tone was apologetic; he was nervous. Evidently the kid was never going to get over being nervous. "I guess I just can't see as straight as you do, Pop."

"Well, dammit, if you'd been careful it would *be* straight. You take enough time, God knows — seems like you could try and do it right." He was tired, and why did he have to explain this? It was obvious. There was no reason why Bob couldn't see it himself.

Bob went on peering upward, rocking back and forth on his heels, his hands in the hip pockets of his paint-spattered jeans. The room was stifling.

"Do you think anyone will really notice? Besides you, I mean."

Carlyle's tongue felt like layers of thick sandpaper. He wanted air. He wanted water. He felt he was nearly choking.

"Do you think anyone will notice? Do you?" He mimicked, in a mincing, high-pitched voice. Almost before he finished saying it, he wished he hadn't. He caught himself and stopped. That was the way he mimicked Helen when she said something stupid.

Bob's flushed face turned white. He took his hands out of his pockets and left the room.

Carlyle stepped off the ladder, pain pulling at his back. He followed Bob out to the driveway. He wanted to smooth the incident over, but the words came from somewhere deep inside him.

"Where do you think you're going? You get back in there and do that job right!"

For one second the boy's eyes met his, swimming blue-green like Helen's eyes. The same blue-green eyes, that couldn't see what they were looking at. Yes, on the fishing trip Carlyle had noticed how like Helen the boy was. Helen's son. Not his.

Bob reached his car, opened the door and stood behind it.

"No, I won't," he said. "*You* paint the room over if you want. I've tried, but I guess I can't do it. You do it yourself, then maybe you'll be satisfied. All you do is insult the people who work for you."

"That's some way to talk," Carlyle began, but Bob got in, slammed the door and started the car. The worn-out engine sounded like an alligator grinding its teeth. "You'll never learn if you act this way," he said, but Bob was gone.

He went inside, breathing the thick air. It would be easier without having to worry about the kid. He stayed late that evening and the next, painting non-stop with the pale tints he had mixed; the tints were so pale it *was* hard to tell where the paints ended and the white ceiling began. He tried not to think about his back and his shoulders. He breathed the strong paint smell, trying not to think at all.

Finally, after three days of hard work, he finished the painting. He left the stucco men at the house and went home. Sarah was packing.

"You going?"

He had not eaten dinner with her the last three nights while he was working so hard. He had eaten out, and left her some money on the kitchen table. He was sure that Bob had told her what had happened and that he had to work hard to finish that job alone.

Her yellow hair was pulled back into a ponytail and tied with a rubber band. She was no nonsense all right, Sarah. She would never have Mary Beaumont's style, but she didn't seem to care much about it.

"Mom's coming home," she said. "I'm picking her up, don't worry about it. She knows you're busy. I thought I'd get my things together now, while I've got time. I'll be leaving later tonight."

"They still didn't find out what it was," he said.

"No, they just eliminated some things." She sounded knowledgeable, almost businesslike. "It's definitely a blood disorder — one of the things, anyway. They're not exactly sure, but they don't think it's serious at this point."

"That's good," he said. He didn't say that he'd said from the first that it wasn't serious. He was too tired to say it.

In his room he undressed and lay down slowly, nursing his back. The sheets were damp in the humid August air but his nose and throat still felt dry. His back hurt so much that he dreaded having to get up again. But he could not sleep so he got up finally, put his clothes back on and went out to the garage and got the rake.

A lot of St. Augustine grass was creeping into his lawn from the minister's property next door. Even though he edged carefully and kept after it, it just didn't seem to want to give up. Tired as he was, he carried the rake into the hot sun and began pulling up the creepers. He pulled first with the rake, and then dropped it, grabbed the creepers with both hands and tugged. The grass rippled as the creeper ripped across the soil. He tugged and pulled on each one, until he was dragging them out of the minister's yard too. Before he could cut them he had to leave them lying there like the dismembered legs of giant spiders across his front lawn. Lines showed where the runners had been pulled up, but that was all right, he had to get rid of them. Some of them were as thick as rope and so hard to pull up that he had to get down painfully on his knees and dig into the soil with his hands. He dug and yanked hard to dislodge the roots from the dirt.

Sarah came up behind him.

"Pop, don't you think you're overdoing it? It's awfully hot out here, and you've been working so hard to get that house done —"

You don't know anything about that house, he thought, you've never seen it.

"Somebody's got to do these things. I can't let St. Augustine take over the front yard just because I had to build a house."

He pulled at a tough creeper and it made a series of almost animal noises as it yanked loose, roots and all, from the earth.

"I went out to the garage, looking for some stuff," Sarah said. He went on digging at the next runner. He wished she would go away.

"I found the table," she said. "I didn't know you had sanded it this summer. When did you ever find the time?"

"We had a lot of rain," he said. "I was cooped up, I had to do something to pass the time."

"Oh, sure," she said. She sounded as though she were smiling. "Listen, why don't you just rest today? The grass isn't going anywhere."

He didn't bother to answer.

"The table looks beautiful," she said.

Why was she hanging around? Why didn't she just leave?

"Thanks for doing it."

He pulled another runner. It sprayed dirt all over him.

"That's okay," he said.

Still she didn't leave.

"You gonna get your mother now?" he asked. He got up slowly, brushing the dirt off his shorts.

She looked at her watch. "Yes, in a minute. And I hope . . ."

Here it came. Another speech. Sarah was good at making speeches.

"You hope what?" he said. "You hope what? What do you hope?"

Her face flushed. In it he saw his own sudden anger. "Oh, nothing!" she cried. "I don't hope anything! What's the use!"

She went back into the house, walking with quick determined strides. Well, she was right about something for once in her life. It wasn't any use.

He hurt his back, hitching the boat trailer to the car, but since he could not sleep and could not paint the stucco on Beaumont's house until it was dry, he decided he would take a six pack and get in some fishing.

The water was calm. He ran the motor until he was well out into the Gulf; then he turned it off and drifted, hearing only the cries of seagulls and the lapping of the waves. His throat itched and his eyes burned; he remembered reading about the red tide. He had not seen any dead fish at the boat ramp, but out here in the water he could tell they were somewhere near, hidden beneath the surface. He opened a can of beer and drank it down. It made his throat feel less raw, not so scratchy.

He drifted a while longer before dropping anchor and casting. It would be stupid to try to catch anything today; he wouldn't want to eat any fish caught during red tide, even though only shellfishing was outlawed. But he cast anyway. He paid little attention to the line, expecting few fish even to strike today. There weren't many other boats out; the three he could see looked like they were already heading for shore. A large cabin cruiser zoomed by, showing no consideration, leaving behind a rough wake.

He drank a second beer and pushed his straw hat farther up on his forehead. It felt wet. He looked at his palm. Sweat. A healthy dose of it. He rubbed the third can of beer against his forehead, letting the cool drops of condensation mingle with his own sweat. It felt good.

He could hardly bear to look at the bright Gulf even in the late afternoon sun; the nearly cloudless sky was a dazzling blue. From time to time he closed his eyes against the glare. He thought of all the brush strokes he had made in the last three days, all the square feet he had covered, inch by inch, with paint. The paint was beautiful—a beautiful covering for a beautiful surface. Paint wasn't meant to hide anything ugly. Beneath the paint in the Beaumont house was solid wall, solid construction, not cheap, flimsy stuff that paint could hide, the way the bright sea hid the ugly red tide. Ugly things would not stay hidden, anyway.

The sun began to go down. He drank his fourth, and then his fifth beer. Fish weren't touching his bait, or maybe he was too sleepy to notice if they did. If Duffy were in the boat with him, he would help him stay awake. Or Bob. Or even Pascagouli. Well, the hell with them all; he didn't need them. He was tired, and it was peaceful here; no people talking. He decided to take the boat out more often. Duffy had always pestered him to do it. He could do it every day when the weather was good. And why not? He wasn't so anxious to go to Johnny's any more, and there were no more houses to build.

His bladder became painfully full. He stood up slowly and urinated into the water. There were no other boats nearby, and anyway he didn't care.

The sunset was dull, as usual with a cloudless sky. By now Sarah would have brought Helen home, and Sarah would probably be flying out soon. Helen would start taking her new medicine, and either she would get well or they would put her back in the hospital. *Nothing serious that they know of.* Some day, of course, there would be something serious and he knew that day wouldn't be long in coming.

The healthy smell of his fresh sweat mingled with the salty air. He could go for a longer fishing trip—maybe three or four days, and breathe that good salty air. Who needed a kid like Bob on a fishing trip? He could go alone. He began to think of turning back now, but his eyelids were heavy and he thought he would just sit for a while with his eyes closed. After he went in and painted the stucco, that would be all he had to do on the Beaumont house. He wouldn't be there to see Mary Beaumont's face when she walked through the rooms and saw his interior work. But he didn't need to see it. He knew she would be pleased and that was all he really needed to know. He put down the rod and dozed in the plastic boat seat with its low back.

He woke in the dark. His feet were wet and cold. He reached his hand down to the floor. Water. The boat was leaking, and he was far from shore. Boatcraft. This was their sloppy work. Angrily, he hauled up the anchor. With luck it would be a slow leak. He started the motor, afraid that now, the one time when he needed it desperately, it would fail. But it kicked over on the first try.

He headed for the lights on land, pushing fear away, but unable to keep the image of drowning out of his mind. When Sarah was little, she trusted only him not to let her drown; he was the only one who could carry her out into the waves and teach her to swim. He had never told anyone, not even Helen, that he was deeply afraid of drowning.

The water was choppy; the boat was going so fast that it smacked hard every second against the waves. He realized that this could cause the leak to get worse and cut the speed slightly. Well, hell. He ought to go ahead and cut the damn thing off. Do them all a favor. He shook his head impatiently. No, he'd never panic and give in, not that way. Carlyle Simpson was not a coward. And that was why they hated him. They got in his way, and they wanted him to change. But even they must know that wasn't going to happen. He was what he was. "Whatever it is," Pascagouli had said, "don't just let it happen." What could a young egghead like that know about *him*? Didn't know anything. "Whatever it is . . ." What was that supposed to mean?

He was beginning to feel sick from the beer; he belched loudly. The wind had picked up; the wet salty air blew against his face. The water in the boat was halfway to his knees. Empty beer cans bobbed like life buoys. He submerged one can, filled it with water and dumped the water overboard. It couldn't help, but he did it anyway.

He was nearing land, but not close enough to see the beach or the boat ramp, although he looked for the markers. He thought he must be a mile or so out. He left the steering lever long enough to locate his tackle box on the other seat. Good; he was afraid it might have fallen into the boat and gotten soaked. He plunged his hands into the water, feeling for the bait bucket. Its cold metal startled him as though he had touched some foreign creature.

The bait bucket was heavy with the water that had filtered in through the tiny holes in its metal cover. He pulled it up, watched the streams of water roll off its top and then opened the lid and dumped the contents overboard. Shrimp and minnows tumbled over each other in a waterfall, back into the Gulf, where they would most probably die. The shells of the shrimp shone translucent pink in the weak moonlight — prettier, much prettier than the delicate tint of pink on the Beaumont's bedroom walls. He reached out and caught up one of the wriggling creatures in his hand. It had tiny legs and eyes; beneath its hard symmetrical surface it was fragile and delicate; he could crush it in an instant. The shell protected, and at the same time imprisoned, the tender, vulnerable mass of its body. A turtle could at least poke its head out of its shell once in a while; these things couldn't. He threw the shrimp into the Gulf where the red tide or something else would kill it.

He had missed the markers and now he did not know where he was. He could see seawall, but no beach. The boat was heading straight for the seawall. He cut the motor and let it drift slowly toward the wall. The way the boat was taking on water, it would be better to go ahead and get to land any way he could, rather than go looking for the ramp and maybe not finding it. He drew up closer to the wall, searching without luck for any opening, even for the steps that were set into the seawalls at intervals. He tried giving the boat a half turn, so he could cruise along the wall before he got too close to it and the boat grounded. He jerked violently on the cord, to try the motor again, but nothing happened. Caught in seaweed, probably.

He felt around in the rising water for the oars and finally found them. They had probably never been used. He waded to the bench in the middle of the boat and set the oars up. But it was useless, the boat would not move. He tried stroke after stroke, working up a good sweat, but the boat would not move. It was too full of water, too close to shore. He pushed one of the oars into the water, thinking he might be able to hit bottom, but he did not. The propellers weren't grounded, but they must have become entrapped in seaweed. The boat would not come loose.

Carefully, he eased himself over the side. First one leg, then the other; he almost tipped the boat over, but he hardly cared any longer whether it sank or not. When he was free of the boat, he pulled himself around to the propellers and tried to free them. But they were deeply entangled in the tough seaweed. He thought he might be able to get them loose if he had all night to work on them, but he could not waste his energy on that stupid boat; he had to get to land. As he took his first broad strokes, he realized how good it felt to be moving away from the boat, to be free of worrying with it. The water buoyed him up, his body felt lighter than it had in years. The pressure was off his back and he could move without pain.

As he neared the seawall, the breaking waves tossed him under, and he took a mouthful of salt water. Spitting and rubbing his burning eyes, he realized that even these small waves could dash him against the wall and crush him. So he began to swim sideways, perpendicular to the waves, hoping to see where the wall ended and the beach began, or at least where an opening was for steps. His hand touched a fish. It was dead. There were others floating near him, victims of the red tide.

He could barely tilt his head to look upward without falling, but he was able to see that the top of the seawall was only a couple of feet above him. He pressed his body against the barnacles and held to them with his left hand. His undershirt, his shorts, caught and tore on the jagged edges. He was glad it was his wet clothes that were catching and tearing and not his flesh.

For a moment he nearly blacked out. He took a deep breath and closed his eyes. He saw Helen at home, snoring in front of the television set; he saw her dragging the heavy bucket of water to pour on his fire, and he saw himself, a soaking wet, sour tub of lard, cut and bleeding. He threw his back, every ounce of strength he could muster, into the thrust and reached the top of the wall, pulling himself up slowly against the concrete, after his right hand grasped the top. There were no barnacles on the wall at this height but the rough concrete scraped the skin off his knees.

Then he was over the wall and lay panting on his stomach in the sand and weeds, not caring that he was picking up the small, painful spurs that grew there. The pain in his back had sharp edges, like knives digging into his spine. He gritted his teeth and a groan escaped him.

He did not know how long he lay there, groaning, his eyes closed, his lips parted. There was sand in his mouth. He was drooling like a baby, and he opened his eyes and wiped a sticky mess from his chin. Finally, he pushed himself up, gasping in pain. He hardly cared about the cuts all over his body, the stinging sand and salt. It was his back that hurt most, every movement felt like hammer blows striking from his neck to his buttocks, and even down his legs. He began to walk very slowly and reached the beach at last. The smell of the red tide was stronger here. Dead fish lay on the sand. The county people would clear them away in the morning, but the tourists would not come to the beach as long as the red tide brought the smell of death. No one would want to be here now, while the red tide threw up rotting fish.

He turned toward the highway, where he knew he would find his way, eventually, to his car. The keys still jangled in his soggy pocket, although his wallet had fallen out. He didn't care about that. Duffy's boat would be sunk before morning. He smiled. The boat didn't mean a damn thing. Houses and boats weren't what was important, not at all. He still tasted salt and sand. He moved his pain-wracked, water-logged body stiffly, but still he felt a strange lightness. Duffy hadn't left him just a boat. Houses, boats, all—he had to learn to let them go, so he could breathe. He flexed the muscles in his bloody arms. Next time he saw Nelson, he'd show him how nasty a wrestler a strong old bastard could be.